QUANTUM LEAP
OUT OF TIME. OUT OF BODY.
OUT OF CONTROL.

The QUANTUM LEAP Series

QUANTUM LEAP
DOUBLE OR NOTHING

A NOVEL BY
C. J. HENDERSON
with
LAURA ANNE GILMAN
BASED ON THE UNIVERSAL TELEVISION
SERIES *QUANTUM LEAP*
CREATED BY DONALD P. BELLISARIO

BOULEVARD BOOKS, NEW YORK

Quantum Leap: Double or Nothing, a novel by C. J. Henderson, based on the Universal television series QUANTUM LEAP, created by Donald P. Bellisario.

QUANTUM LEAP: DOUBLE OR NOTHING

A Boulevard Book/published by arrangement with MCA Publishing Rights, a Division of MCA, Inc.

PRINTING HISTORY
Boulevard edition/December 1995

ISBN: 1-57297-055-3

BOULEVARD
Boulevard Books are published by The Berkley Publishing Group,
200 Madison Avenue, New York, New York 10016.
BOULEVARD and its logo
are trademarks belonging to Berkley Publishing Corporation.

PRINTED IN THE UNITED STATES OF AMERICA

10 9 8 7 6 5 4 3 2

With due gratitude and humble thanks to
Ginjer Buchanan, editor of patience,
and
Ashley McConnell, who understood

—*LAG*

To be nobody but yourself—in a world which is doing its best, night and day, to make you everybody else—means to fight the hardest battle which any human being can fight, and never stop fighting.

—e.e. cummings

I have never seen a greater monster or miracle in the world than myself.

—Montaigne

PROLOGUE

Dr. Sam Beckett had made a lot of Leaps by the first time he arrived at the tenth of May, 1986.

Although each Leap was different, he always knew the moment history was put back to rights. He had come to recognize the end of his intrusion in someone's life the way a symphony conductor can *feel* a concert's approaching finale—instinctively, without looking at the music.

As if the last cymbal crash had just been completed, Sam felt the moment of completeness slipping over him. Part of him, as always, warmed to the bright tingle that precipitated the coming lunge Outward. And, also as always, another part of him resented it, wondering when his days of Leaping would be over, and he would be returned to his own life. But Dr. Sam Beckett hadn't been in charge of this Project in a long time, and he had learned to take what satisfaction he could from a job well done, and not think too much about what he couldn't change.

As the familiar shimmer rose to envelope him, he first lost sight of Al, then the rest of his surroundings. Everything felt as it always did. His anticipation grew, his borrowed eyes closing, his borrowed mouth curved into a smile. Leaping had become like skiing to Sam—lean into the curves, push off for speed, bend into the wind—all downhill and easy.

Piece of cake, he thought. Nothing to it.

And normally, he would have been correct. But this time . . . this time he was wrong. In that fraction of a second he had in between bodies—in between lives—he felt a sudden jagged agony that tore his eyes open and split his mouth into a piercing scream.

His eyes burned from the exploding torment, locking on the ceiling of the Waiting Room.

The Waiting Room? asked a tiny part of his mind. What was he doing there?

The part of him that could even notice his surroundings wondered if at long last he might have finally made it back home. The rest of his brain was forced to ignore the question; it was too busy shutting down nerve bunches, silencing a thousand requests for relief every millisecond.

Sam's mouth locked open during his return—paralyzed wide and round—by his body's need to scream. It was an instinctive response, his primate brain overwhelming the more sophisticated layers above it in order to deal with the flooding rush of searing agony. His rational mind in shreds, the cortex was taking over, trying

2

to use mere noise to chase away the racking, brutal pain. It did not work.

His body had been standing when he had reentered it. His newly crippled presence sent it flying, toppling—spasms of misery punishing him so severely he could not feel the additional sting as his face slammed against the wall.

Nor did he feel the grueling hurt of what followed, not of his knees hitting the floor—left first, then the right—not the crack of his right shoulder or the sting of his head. Indeed, by that point he was already gone, leaving those simple pains for whoever entered his body next.

This wasn't a Leap, it was a sundering. The fabric of his soul was tied in knots, turned inside out, and then ripped in half. For the first time, his passage through the Ether had become a fall into hell. His pain was so great that he could not think, could not breathe, could not even comprehend what thinking or breathing might be.

And then, it was over. The split second of a usually glorious Leap had become a nightmare ended. The actual pain gone, its residual presence dug into Sam's nerve endings with sharp-edged fingers, tearing at him with every breath, every thought.

Sam stayed curled within the brain of his new host for a long time, not caring who, or where, or when. He was afraid to move, afraid to breathe, afraid to think. On the most basic level, Sam Beckett was terrified that once he did any of the three the pain would start again.

He was right.

3

CHAPTER
ONE

After an unmeasured space of time had gone by, Sam finally opened his eyes, very slowly. There was an intense throbbing in his head, but nothing to compare with what he had experienced before.

Well, he thought, that didn't hurt nearly as much as I thought it was going to.

Sam inventoried his new body, probing for any other lingering signs of the pain he had felt during the Leap that had brought him to ... where? A quick survey of his surroundings told him that he was not in the Waiting Room. For whatever reason he had briefly flashed there, he had left again, finding his way once again to some other time, some other body, some other problem to be solved.

"Damn," he cursed, anger the overriding emotion flooding his mind. "Damnit, anyway. Here we go again."

Sam wondered at his instinctive reaction. Sure, he often felt frustration over not being able to get back to his own life. But never before had he felt such bitterness.

Of course, he told himself, never before had he come so close to making it back, either. He thought for a while about what possible fluctuation might have brought him back to the Waiting Room, but soon pushed the question aside. For all he knew, he had appeared in the Waiting Room a thousand times before. His memory had developed so many different holes through his various Leaps, it would not have surprised him to find out that he had only had one peaceful Leap and all the rest had been horribly painful experiences like the one he had just ridden out.

Taking stock in his situation, Sam looked around his latest host's room.

Hey, I'm in bed, he thought. Now that, *that* is a nice change.

Sam tried out the muscles of his new face, seeing how they felt when he smiled, deciding they molded into a smile just fine. What a blessed relief to open his eyes, for once—and not be staring out at an audience waiting for him to perform. Or in a battle zone.

Or pregnant, he thought, stretching his arms over his head. Or—oh, hell—a chimp. He remembered those Leaps, if not the details of them.

No, for once it was nice to just wake up like a normal guy in a normal bed in a normal room. Chuckling to himself, he stretched again, thinking that if he had to keep Leaping, this was the way he wanted to do it. His mind ran back to a sudden memory—a cartoon he had seen somewhere, in his own past or some previous Leap, showing an overweight, white-mustached man lounging by the pool in workout sweats. Next to him was a tuxedo-clad butler, puffing and sweating, doing sit-ups. The punch line had read, ''Hurry up and do those sit-ups, Jeeves. I've got to get into shape.''

Yeah, thought Sam, grinning to himself. That's the ticket. Low maintenance Leaping from now on. No muss, no fuss. No punches in the head. Just get up out of bed and go down and read the morning paper.

Then a sudden thought struck him. What if his new host couldn't get out of bed? What if he had no legs, or was dying, or . . .

Pushing aside his paranoia, Sam jumped out from under the sheet and blanket, hitting the floor with a satisfying thud. He looked around the room, searching out clues to his new life. The walls were papered in a light blue print of small flowers—tasteful and reserved and not, Sam felt, the pick of his host.

The overhead light fixture was off-the-shelf. The dresser, secondary dresser, the chair next to them, nightstand . . . all had the same thrift-shop look to them. They were well chosen, and they had all been refinished by a careful if inexpert hand. Sam sized his new self up as lower middle class, but trying.

The room lacked all but the simplest, most basic adornments. There was a mirror and two posters on the walls—one of a country band, another of the Harley-Davidson symbol, but nothing else. No fish tank, flowers, pictures, no books. His host seemed to be a man of few belongings.

6

The nightstand had a bargain-basement reading lamp and several magazines, but Sam noted they did not seem to be on his side of the bed. No, his side of the bed showed him only a pack of Marlboros with three cigarettes remaining and an empty Jack Daniel's bottle.

Huuummmmm, he thought, holding the bottle up to the window, checking to see if it was recently emptied or merely long forgotten. Spotting several wet drops still sliding freely around the inside he put his hand to his head again, concluding, This might explain my headache. Oh, boy, is it a doozy.

Sam set the bottle back down on the floor next to the cigarettes and crossed the room to the mirror. He looked himself over, pleased with what he saw. He was a tall man; over six feet, well muscled, with broad shoulders and a thick neck.

And not bad-looking, either. That's a nice plus. I mean, all right, next time I'll be a balding, one-legged dwarf with an eye patch, but this time—he smiled into the mirror, checking his straight teeth—*not bad.*

Staring into the blue-gray eyes of his reflection, he flexed the muscles of one arm, then both, then ran his fingers through his shoulder-length black hair.

"No, not bad at all."

Searching for something to wear, he checked the closet first. He found what appeared to be his clothes on one side and a large number of empty hangers on the other. He raised one eyebrow at the sight, wondering what would make whoever he was keep his house that way. Then he decided to worry about it after he found out who he was and what his chore was to be this time.

7

Pulling out a pair of black jeans, he carried them with him to the large dresser. While he searched for some underwear and socks and a shirt, he talked to himself in a whisper.

"So, who are you, buddy? And what's your problem? What's God, Time, or Whoever got in mind for me this time around? Man, you build one little Quantum Accelerator and throw yourself out into time . . . and this is the thanks you get."

Sam stopped, wondering at his own words. Ever since waking up in his new body, he had seemed more at odds with his Leaping than ever before.

Pulling a pair of bikini briefs out of the dresser's top drawer, along with a pair of socks, he said aloud, "Maybe it's this headache. This Leap was worse than usual, I think."

Shrugging, Sam put on the briefs and socks, and then pulled his pants on. Spotting a pair of cowboy boots on the side of the dresser, he sat down on the edge of the bed and put them on as well. A part of his mind wondered if his host tucked his pant legs in or pulled them over his boots.

This time, as so often in the past, instinct took over, and Sam found himself tucking the pant legs into the boots. He sat back, finding himself agreeing with the choice. No, he, Sam Beckett, was not one for cowboy boots, and on those occasions where he had worn them he had always preferred his pants on the outside, but this time, tucked felt just right.

Sam stood up, noticing again the empty bottle on the floor next to the cigarettes.

"Well," he said, picking up the bottle, "maybe *this* is what made it a bad Leap."

He could not be certain, not with the Leaps making Swiss cheese out of his memory, but perhaps being drawn into a drunk was what had caused such severe pain this time. Maybe alcohol set up some sort of barrier that made Leaping particularly painful.

"Could be that's all it was—Leaping into a hangover." If so, he hoped his host, back in the Waiting Room, had a headache to match his. Dropping the bottle into the wastebasket near the door, he said, "Well, if that *is* all that's ruining my day, I won't have to worry about it ruining any more."

Although, as the bottle left his fingers, Sam felt a twinge of regret run through his new body. It happened often. During almost every Leap he could feel the needs of his host crying out, struggling with him to do things in certain ways even though they were no longer present—consciously or unconsciously.

As far as Sam knew, if he were to splash some water on his face and brush his teeth, he could probably get rid of or at least lessen the hangover still nagging his new brain. But that was the least of his problems right now. Priority one: who was he? He scanned the room again, looking for a pair of pants rolled up somewhere that might have a wallet or some other key to his identity.

Nothing.

Sam did not like the idea of going out into the hall without some idea of what his name was.

Why couldn't you have framed a birthday card

someone gave you, or have won a bowling trophy, or *something*, huh, buddy?

A bit of scribble on the country western poster caught Sam's eye. Crossing the room again, he bent over and read, *Best wishes from The Gallagher Gang to Ward and Betty.*

"Ward," he whispered. "All right, Ward, let's go get you cleaned up."

Betty, Sam thought. He noticed that he was wearing a wedding ring. Studying its design for a second, he added, "Yeah. Let's go get cleaned up, meet Betty, and get this show on the road."

His hand on the doorknob, Sam stopped to wonder where Al was. A shard of memory flashed from his painful last Leap. It had been night. He had first entered Ward's body at night.

Looking around for a clock, not finding one, Sam went to the window. Sticking his head out, he looked up. He had learned to tell time during his boyhood days in the country.

"It's nine," he said aloud. "At least nine. But it was dark when I Leaped in. Even, even if it was almost sunrise—I've been here for . . . for what? Four, five hours already."

Where's Al? He's always here by now.

The thought unnerved Sam. Yes, Al had been late on some occasions, or had waited until Sam could talk freely. But Sam could certainly talk freely here in the bedroom by himself, and Al might have been late before, but never this late.

At least, not that I can remember.

10

And that was it, wasn't it? That was always it. Every new Leap he had to start over from scratch, learning what he did—and didn't—remember. Maybe it had taken Al days to reach him in the past. Maybe he had bad Leaps every time he turned around. Maybe Ward was causing problems somehow—if he really was Ward. Maybe Ward was the husband of some woman his host had spent the night with, and now Sam was going to have to explain his way out of another hopelessly ludicrous situation.

He growled to himself.

I get the idea. Leaping is tough. Well, I knew the job was dangerous when I took it.

Let's assume the best case scenario. Our name is Ward; this is our home. We're a pretty basic type of guy which, along with being a smoker and a drinker, means we've got some kind of basic problem to fix up and then we'll be out here. So . . .

Sam let his new fingers grip the doorknob again, letting them turn it this time. He pushed the door open and stepped out into the hall.

Buck up, Sam, he thought. Maybe Al's late, maybe he isn't. Who cares? Whatever's going on, we'll handle it. Something will change for some guy named Ward, we'll Leap into the next job, and that'll be the end of it. Easy.

"Right?" he asked the air in the hallway, answering, "Of course, right."

CHAPTER
TWO

The door to the Control Room crashed open, accompanied by a dry, growling voice screaming questions.

"What is this? I can't take a lousy nap without this place falling apart around me? This had all better be somebody's idea of a sick joke. That's all it is, right?"

Banging his way into the chamber under full steam was Admiral Al Calavicci. His usually dark eyes were darker than normal, each of them sporting bags underneath black enough to match the bushy eyebrows above. He had been trying to catch up on at least a few of the dozen hours of sleep he had lost over the last two months trying to keep track of Sam.

"Just an hour," he had pleaded. Of course, being Al Calavicci, even when he had begged for "just one little hour, sixty tiny little minutes so I can try and get my feet back under me" his gravel-shod voice had made it sound much more like an order than a plea.

Still, he had tried so hard to sound reasonable that everyone involved had sworn they would not bother him unless there was a real need. But he had not gotten an hour. Although he had fallen asleep within twenty seconds of closing his eyes, it had only been twelve minutes before a panicking Dr. Beeks was shaking him awake.

Al's first reaction was to throw a fit. His nerves were certainly egging him on. Every muscle in his body was tight, almost spastic. He had missed too much sleep, drunk too much coffee, skipped too many meals, and had basically abused himself in the name of the Project.

But then his eyes focused on Verbeena Beeks's. He saw the fear on her face—not something he saw there often. He also felt the urgency in her grip, the way the tips of her fingers were digging into his arms. This was not the Verbeena Beeks he knew. And so, as much as he was loath to do so, he crawled out from under his jacket that had been doubling as a blanket. Wiping his eyes clear, he staggered to his feet and made his way to Ziggy, the incredibly advanced hybrid computer in the heart of the Project.

And now he stood there, staring at the slightly left-of-center section of the main panel of the Quantum Project's computer he always thought of as the machine's face.

"What in all the rings of hell do you mean you don't have a fix on Sam yet?" he demanded.

"I do not think there is any point in raising your voice, Admiral."

"Etiquette lessons, Ziggy?" sputtered the admiral. "Sonofabitch, why should I care what you think?"

13

"Nor is there any need for risqué language. Let us review the simple facts," came the computer's voice. "I am no one's son, human, canine, or any other. I am a construct. A very expensive and highly intelligent one. Which is why you care very much what I think. That answering your second question, I will now answer your first."

Al fought the tension in his balled fists. He told himself that it was only his nerves—just the fatigue making him angry—not the exasperating machine in front of him. Al knew if he did not get his fingers unclenched he would end up smashing them against the computer, which would help no one.

Bottling up the various frustrations once again, Al cut off his anger, blocking it out in every way he had ever learned. He jammed his hands into his pockets to keep them from throttling too-smart computers and started again, speaking as calmly as possible.

"Okay, okay. You're right, and I'm wrong. There's no need for tension, so . . . so I'm not tense. So, go ahead, answer my question. What's all this about not being able to locate Sam?" he asked Ziggy.

"I do not believe you are actually calm."

"That doesn't matter, Ziggy," answered Al through a clenched smile. "Just tell me about Sam."

"There are two distinct veins visible on your forehead which are normally not noticeable. This indicates—"

"It indicates that you're driving me *nuts*, you pile of scrap!" growled Al. Picking up a clipboard from a desk next to him, the only thing in the room of any substance, he waved it at the left-of-center spot, shouting, "It indicates I'm about to slap you upside your nonexistent head if you don't stop dancing around and get to the point!''

Al flung the clipboard and its papers away. They hit the door through which he had just entered, the board breaking and the papers spilling across the floor. Al closed his eyes and his mouth, running his fingers through his hair, trying to get control of himself.

Too much, he told himself. This has been going on too long. It's just too much.

He shook his head violently, chasing away the depression and the fuzziness that had invaded his brain. Lifting his head, he opened his eyes and stared at Ziggy.

''You're stalling,'' he told the machine in a much calmer voice. When the computer failed to respond, Al went on the attack. ''You can't find Sam, and you don't want to talk about it, because you don't want to admit it.''

Ziggy remained silent. Colored cubes of light continued to flash on and off within the Control Room. Pointing to them, Al said, ''You've broken off most of yourself and sent it looking for him, and you've just got some tiny little bit here trying to hold me off. It's not going to work this time, Zigster.''

''I am not stalling, Admiral,'' replied the computer.

''Oh, no? Oh, no? No good, Ziggy. No damn good. I might not have designed you like Sam did, or actually cemented all your neurocells in place like Tina, so I might not know you as well as they do, but after all the time we've had to spend together, I've got your number down pretty good.''

"You do not understand," came the soft female voice of the computer. "I am not stalling, Admiral."

"No? What would you call it, then?"

"I have already admitted that I cannot locate Dr. Beckett. If your hypotheses were correct, I would not have made that admission at all."

Al cooled down a bit, wondering what Ziggy was up to. Sometimes he didn't trust the supercomputer. They had wrangled too many times in the past. Al was not arrogant enough to believe he could out-think Ziggy no matter how much the machine galled him. He had tripped her up in the past, but it had taken effort. However, Al reminded himself yet again, she was still a computer—fast at pulling together facts and lightning when juggling figures. She could extrapolate and produce theories, but wit, along with some of the human brain's other companion skills, was still a bit beyond her. Thanks to Sam she was closer to human than any computer had ever been before. But she was *not* human.

Thus, Al always fought to the end, never wanting to make any of Ziggy's all too frequent victories any easier for her than they had to be. And Ziggy played the same game. It was what they did, to give Al some sense of control over a Project gone ca-ca. Still, the admiral did not sense any of the usual tones the machine used whenever she was looking to outmaneuver him.

Wondering what she was up to, he admitted, "No, no, you wouldn't. Okay, Zig, I'll bite. Here I am, concerned but calm. So tell me. Why can't you find Sam?"

"Because I am sick."

Of all the possible answers Al had prepared himself for, that one had not even been on the list.

CHAPTER
THREE

Sam moved out into the hall, hitting a loudly creaking board with his first step. Before he could lift his foot again he opened his senses, concentrating on the rest of the house. Immediately he heard some slight reaction to the noise coming from downstairs.

Nuts, thought Sam, wondering what was happening below him. As always, the subconscious level of his brain had already begun noting basic facts—rapidly weaving questions and then answering them.

In seconds it noted that Sam was on a second level with no upward staircase—okay, we're in a two-story house. The furnishings in the hall, as well as those he could see down the stairs and in the other rooms, all of it was consistent with the design style he had noted in the bedroom—high probability we're the owner, not a renter. His head craned down, showing him that the hall had throw rugs, not wall-to-wall—warm climate. Native

American weaving—could possibly indicate that I'm somewhere in the western United States . . .

While the rote computer part of his brain worked on the more mundane aspect of where he was, Sam's conscious mind concentrated on the practical and the immediate; drawing conclusions from the noise he had heard below when he had stepped on the board.

It had been a gasp. Not a sound of pleasure that he was awake, or even one of exasperation that he was *finally* awake, but one of trepidation . . . fear.

Someone's doing something they don't want me to know about. The question is, are they planning a surprise party or robbing me blind?

An inner feeling, the one Sam had come to trust throughout his Leaping, told him that it was neither. But, it told him, he should certainly get himself downstairs. Fast.

"Oh, well," he whispered, noticing for the first time Ward's thick, Western accent, " 'Once more into the breech, dear friends, once more . . .' "

Letting the quote trail off, Sam headed for the stairs, taking them two at a time. At the bottom, across the house's small foyer, he spotted a mismatched set of luggage, including several shopping bags and a cardboard box. Working on moving the load out the propped-open front door, he found a young girl, blond, perhaps ten years old, and a woman who was either her young mother or her older sister.

"Hey," asked Sam, using the most noncommittal tone he could, "what's goin' on?"

Don't want to sound like an idiot—this could be any

number of trips I'm supposed to know about. They may even be getting things ready while they wait for Ward to snap out of his stupor.

Reasonable assumptions, the kind Sam had to make whenever he first felt his way through a Leap, but that inner feeling told him he knew what was going on. Focusing his attention on their eyes, he knew it was right.

They're running away.

From me.

"Don't you try and stop us, Ward, you shit," the woman said. Sam looked at her, studying her for whatever clues he could get to help him figure out what was happening. She was blond, like the girl, green-eyed, and strongly built, standing a good, solid height, five-nine, ten, maybe. Her accent clued him further to his location. That, the rug, his glimpse out the window—he was somewhere in the Pacific Northwest.

Somewhere in that few thousand square miles, he was faced off with an attractive woman—my wife?—who was running away from him—with my child?—because he was—a shit?

Oh, yeah, this is going to be easy.

"Sweetheart," he started, his voice stumbling. Damn, he thought, what do I say to her? What can I say? What's our relationship? What's right—what's not going to make me sound like an idiot?

The blond woman stood defiantly before him, shielding the luggage as much as the girl. Before anyone could say anything further, another child came through the door—a boy, older than the girl, his hair darker, his face cut from the same lines Sam had seen in the mirror.

19

Stealing a quick glance at the woman's left hand, he spotted a wedding ring matching his own.

Yeah, your wife, and—his eyes flashed to the dark-haired boy again—and your kids. You'd better do something. And whatever it is, it'd better be quick.

"Betty," he said, crossing his fingers he was interpreting his clues correctly. "Why?"

"You have to ask?" the woman replied. "You can't think of any reasons on your own why we'd all want to get the hell away from you as far and as fast as possible?"

"Maybe I can," he said, desperately searching for a way to get the young woman to do all the talking. "But if I nail myself to the door, how am I ever gonna know if I'm payin' for the right sins?"

Betty turned her back to him. The boy moved in between her and Sam while she reached for another bag, blocking his father's way to his mother. Sam flinched in surprise. Ward, he told his host, you must have really screwed things up around here.

"Son," he said aloud, trying to slow what he saw unfolding before him. "Do you think that's necessary?" Before the boy could answer, Sam backed off a step, trying to defuse the anger he could see welling in the boy's dark eyes.

"Do you think I'd hurt your mother? Or your sister? Or you, even. For that matter?"

"Would if you could," he answered coldly. "Guess you got too drunk last night. Now I figure you're just too hungover to start swinging."

"Taylor," said the woman. "Don't talk to your father that way."

"Don't side with him again, Mom," snapped the boy, a thin line of fear sliding through the anger in his voice. "You said we were leavin' this time for sure."

Betty put her hand on her son's shoulder. He was at least sixteen, and almost as tall as his father. The back of Sam's mind had already started to size up Taylor's physical capabilities, if the two of them were to come to blows. His mother took the reins of the conversation, however, ignoring Taylor's question, addressing Sam instead.

"I'm surprised you were even able to drag yourself out of bed this early. You put away enough last night to keep you out until dinnertime. I thought we'd be halfway to . . . I thought we'd be long gone by the time you staggered your way . . ."

Sam studied Betty, trying to decide how close to the edge she was. He noted her stumble, how she had almost slipped and given away where they were headed. But she had caught herself.

She's not giving her ace-in-the-hole to you, you drunk. But she wants to. You can save this situation, but you'd better get started.

He hesitated. He could almost hear a voice inside his head, a whisper.

Why? it asked. Why even bother? Just so we can Leap again? And again? And again? Maybe if we give up on this crap it'll just stop. It's just a theory, remember? We don't have any proof that time has to be fixed and that we're the only sap capable of fixing it. Or do you *want*

21

to keep Leaping again and again—again and again and again and again?

Sam squeezed his eyes shut, lifting his hands to his ears as if he could stop the noise of his own brain. Trying to turn the situation around, he said honestly, "There's a voice in my head, tellin' me I should just let you go. That if I was to just wave good-bye, that all my problems would be solved. But I don't want to do that."

"Oh, no, Ward?" Betty asked. "And why is that? Tell us the reason. Or wait—maybe you should just let us guess."

Stepping past Taylor, Betty moved up to within an even foot of Sam's face. She stopped there, not coming closer, seemingly afraid to touch him, yet the look on her face was that of a prosecutor about to demolish one last alibi.

She's waiting for me to do or say something, Sam thought. Well, let's just hope I don't do or say it.

"I know the only things you'll miss," she spat out when he didn't say anything. "You'll miss having meals cooked for you. You'll miss the wash getting done, and you'll miss having someone to drive to the store to pick up your smokes and your beer and your booze. That's all you'll miss."

"You don't think I'd miss you, Betty?" Sam tried. "You don't think I'd miss my own kids?"

"No, Ward," answered the woman, the space between them closing by several inches. "No, I don't. What are any of us to you that a punching bag couldn't replace?"

Sam tried to speak but Betty ran over his words,

shouting, "When's the last time you showed any interest in Taylor or Barbara? When's the last time you showed any interest in anything around here outside of getting drunk or getting laid?"

Oh, Ward, my friend, Sam thought in disgust, you're sounding better and better all the time. Grateful to the woman for giving him the name of his daughter, he also found himself wondering—Where are you, Al? I mean, do you have any intention of showing up at all? Because, oh, boy, do I need you!

But the Observer didn't come gliding through the invisible door, his link to Ziggy in hand, to save the day. Sam was on his own.

"Betty"—focus on her name—focus on her—"there isn't much I can say now, is there? You're right about everything. I mean, everything you're sayin', well, that's me, now isn't it? You want me to say that I ain't been good for much, right? Well, all right—I ain't been good for much."

Betty froze. Obviously she had been waiting for a slap, a punch, curses, any one last nail to seal the coffin of her marriage. Sam could tell that she didn't know what to make of his reactions. Maybe she was remembering an earlier Wade? He tried that approach.

"I used to be better. I could be better again." When she did not respond, the cajoling words continued, insisting, "I had to be better somewhere back down the road. You're not stupid enough to have married a guy as bad as me, you just made the mistake of lettin' the guy you married turn into me."

"Don't buy it, Mom," interrupted Taylor, his words

23

bitter with distrust. "He's just talkin' a bunch of country music crap at ya." Turning toward his father, the boy barked, "Whose song you stealin' this time to get over?"

Deal with the boy later, Sam told himself. Work on the wife. If she leaves, they all leave, and you don't have the faintest idea where they're going.

"Betty, I hate soundin' like some kind of daytime TV show or somethin', but I can't let this family break up. Bad as I've been for all of you, if you leave, nothin's gonna be better for any of us. You know what'll happen to me without you. And I figure you've thought plenty enough about what'll happen to the three of you. All I can ask is—is it worth it? I mean, is it worth it to walk out the door, right this minute, and not give me another chance?"

"Jeez, Mom," cried Taylor, the overriding sound in his voice one of pure fright.

Betty stood shaking, which jangled the ring of keys in her hand. Sam listened to them banging against each other, not knowing what else to do. Damnit! Where was Al? He had no idea what he was supposed to change. None at all.

Was he supposed to get the family back together? Wife with husband? Father with son? Without Al and Ziggy, he had no way of knowing. Maybe they had to leave and he had to do something all by himself. Maybe he was supposed to make sure they left—maybe keeping them there would eventually get them killed by a drunken Ward.

I hate this. I really, really, hate this. Whose bright

24

idea was it to bounce me all through time toying with the cosmic matrix? Why do I have to be the one to fix everything? What does it matter, anyway? Maybe after all this time the cosmos can't be put back together. Not by me, anyway. Why can't I just go home?

The need to cry suddenly filled Sam Beckett. He had been going from Leap to Leap for so long—for longer than he could remember. Because of Al's refusal to give him any information about the life he'd left behind—at his own insistence, Sam reminded himself bitterly—he had no idea how long he had been away from the Quantum Project, away from home.

Was it years? Was it?

There was no answer, not from God, or Fate, or Time, or Whoever. His hands balled into fists. Before he could catch hold of himself, before he could think to try, Sam's tears began to fill Ward's eyes, spilling down his unshaven cheeks. He took his fist and swung it at the side of his head, slamming himself harder than he had ever struck at anyone. Ward's body rocked, stumbling sideways. His other fist came up from the opposite direction, hitting him just as hard.

That blow was too much, knocking Sam sideways and backward. He fell against the steps, hitting his shoulder and the back of his head against the wall. Betty cried out and moved forward, her first instinct to stop him from hurting himself. Barbara, silent until that moment, cried out as well, moving to her father's side. Taylor, unimpressed, stood his ground.

"Nice dodge, Dad. I'd really thought you'd blown it this time. I really didn't think you had it in you to get them back—again.'' Crossing his hands across his chest, Taylor stared contemptuously at his mother's back.

"I guess women really are as stupid as you always told me they are.''

Taylor turned his back on all of them and kicked the screen door open. Storming outside, he disappeared from view before anyone could think to stop him.

On the steps, dazed by the force of his own blows, Sam wondered what had prompted his actions. It had made a good show for Betty and Barbara, but he knew he had not been playing the penitent husband for them.

Sam Beckett had been beating on Sam Beckett, for the crime of bothering to care about Leaping and those he Leaped into.

Why, he wondered, more frightened over what was going on inside him than he ever had been at anything else. What's the matter with me?

Racking sobs welled up from within him, forcing more tears down his face. A cold part of his mind watched Betty trying to comfort him. It knew she had been convinced of his sincerity. No one wailed and cried the way he was just for show. But that section of his brain, with its sympathy for Betty, was not the only one speaking to him at that moment.

Another part was agreeing with Taylor, that women really were stupid. That they were easily manipulated. And that part had him frightened, more than his bad Leap, more than the nonappearance of Al, more than anything in his entire life.

Very, very frightened.

26

CHAPTER FOUR

Al sat across the table from Tina and Gushie. None of them looked very good. Al was still suffering from the fatigue that had been dragging him down for months. Tina and Gushie's problems sprang from the chaos at hand.

Ziggy was claiming to be "sick." With Sam gone, as chief programmer, Gushie was the closest thing the computer had to a specialist. As the design engineer who had taken Sam's original dream and made it as real as possible, Tina was the closest thing Ziggy had to a general practitioner.

"Okay, okay—one of you tell me what Her Mental Majesty is talking about? What the hell does it mean—it's sick?"

"We're still not sure, Al," said Tina. Gushie cut the hot-tempered admiral off, adding, "We have an idea. Something has ripped apart her basic AI functions. Split them down the middle, so to speak. We sort of know what *kind* of sick Ziggy is, we just don't know how she got infected.''

''What are you talking about?''

''Somehow,'' answered Tina, taking over for a stumbling Gushie, ''Ziggy's ability to correlate information, to transfer blocks of data, to even give herself commands, has all been . . . I don't know, canceled.''

It was no secret that Gushie, like most of the staff, liked to stay out of Al's way. It was also no secret that Al was soft on Tina. No matter how the changes in the past changed the present, Al could always be counted on to go easier on the beautiful engineer than anyone else. Which was why she had grown used to fielding his outbursts whenever someone else was in the line of fire.

She felt sorry for the admiral at that moment, actually. It was also no secret around the base how hard Al had been pushing himself for quite some time. Much harder than ever before. It had seemed to him for a while that Dr. Beckett was on the verge of making it back to the Project. But the notion had passed, however, leaving the admiral worn to a frazzle, tired, and hollow.

Seeing him trying to face this latest problem, her heart went out to him. No one in the Project worked as hard as he did trying to get Dr. Beckett back. Now, with Ziggy off line, he was more worried than usual. Following up her first statement, she told him, ''Let me give you an example. Say you want to pick up a glass of water. Your brain gives your fingers an order, and you pick the glass up. But right now, Ziggy can't get the message from her brain to her fingers.''

28

"More than that," said Gushie, daring to reenter the conversation. "Ziggy's brain still knows what a glass of water is, but her eyes don't recognize one. Fundamentally, her brain still understands up from down, but she can't tell you which one is which. The connections have been, been"—the programmer waved his hands helplessly—"I don't know. I don't know what they have been."

"Can't we just replace the connections?" asked Al wearily, staring at Tina with hopeful eyes.

"No. I'm sorry. That's what Gushie's been trying to explain. It isn't as if a series of physical, manufactured connectors has cracked or burned out. It just isn't any kind of hardware *or* software problem we've ever come up against before—not with Ziggy, or, or . . . anywhere. It's . . ."

The young woman stopped, not sure where to go next. She knew what she wanted to say, but was not at all sure she could say it to the admiral. Not that she was afraid he would blow up at her—even if he did, she was fully ready to handle him. Tina Martinez-O'Farrell had been handling men for a long time. Even admirals were no real problem for her. No, it was more along the line of not knowing if he could comprehend what she wanted to explain.

After all, she thought, if I can't really explain it to myself, how am I supposed to explain it to anyone else?

"It's what, Tina?" asked Al, his voice betraying a part of the desperation that was beginning to overtake him. Catching a bit of its desperate tone focused Tina's attention. She knew Al Calavicci too well. Desperate was not something in his standard field equipment set.

What could have him tied up in knots that bad? she wondered. Sure, we can't get in touch with Sam, and we've got a problem with Ziggy we've never had before. But still . . .

The admiral yelled. The admiral demanded. The admiral pushed people to the limit, exasperated everyone from technicians to senators, and worked miracles on every third Thursday. But the admiral never worried. Never got desperate. Never panicked.

Never.

Why, Tina asked herself, is it so different this time?

A quick glance at Gushie told Tina that the programmer had not picked up the same vibes. She was tempted to chalk Al's concern up to a combination of their problem with Ziggy and his extreme lack of rest. She knew deep inside that anyone else would be willing to accept that answer.

But that's not Al, she thought nervously. It's not. There's something more wrong here than he's letting on.

Tina took a deep look into Al's eyes, seeing something she did not wish to see. Fear. Hidden away, but there nonetheless. He was afraid. Terrified. Suddenly Tina found herself growing very quiet—and very frightened.

My Lord, nothing scares him. But if something is— scaring him—what could it be? And what does that mean for the rest of us if he can't handle it?

She wasn't sure she wanted to know.

"I said," Al repeated, "it's what, Tina?"

"Oh," the young engineer caught herself, pulling her

mind back to their conversation. "I'm sorry. I got distracted, ah, just thinking about how to explain . . . it's not that I think you can't understand what I want to say. I don't know what it is I want to say." The woman pointed at her head, saying, "The idea is in here, but I can't really hear it yet." She looked at Al plaintively. Then, reaching across the table, she suddenly took his hand in hers and squeezed his fingers, telling him, "But I'll get it, okay? I will. Or Gushie will. Or you will. We're going to beat this."

Looking even more deeply into his eyes, beyond the beginning signposts of fear she had seen earlier, Tina dug down to the Al she knew, the one she respected and, sometimes, even felt more for, and told him, "We will."

Al found himself embarrassed by Tina's attention. He understood, and he was grateful on one level. But ordinarily Al Calavicci did not admit to failure, or fear, and on another level, he resented needing comforting. Still— just that once—Al patted Tina's hand with his free one, then removed it. Switching to his charming voice, the one that came naturally after a life filled with five wives and an infinite number of women he considered as try-outs for the position, he said, "I accept that theory. We haven't let Sam down yet, and we're not going to this time."

Sitting back in his chair, Al took a deep breath, forcing oxygen to his fatigued brain. Taking a long pull from the oversize hot mug he had brought with him to the meeting, he tasted the coffee as it went down, wishing he dared to splash a couple of fingers of Amaretto into it.

It'd be nice, but got to keep going now.

Placing the mug back on the table, Al turned back to the Project's chief engineer and programmer and asked them, "Okay. Let's get started. I want you two to treat me like a senator and go over how the whole system works." When Gushie and Tina just stared, he said, "In a nutshell. But you know how it is, maybe as you explain the system, something one of you says will spark an idea. Sometimes it just takes saying something out loud to have it suddenly make sense."

"Ah, nutshell?" said Gushie. "You step into the Accelerator, and you get propelled back in time."

"Okay," said Al, letting his lips twist into a half grin, half grimace, "maybe I should have said a big nutshell."

"A big nutshell?" said Gushie. "I guess you start with Dr. Beckett at the Star Bright Project when he first noticed that if he took Hawking's work and integrated it with both the research Lofti Zadeh did on fuzzy logic and his own theories that he developed at M.I.T. under Professor LoNigro."

A part of Al's mind listened, searching for a clue as to what might be going on with their multibillion-dollar hybrid computer, for any suggestion he might make that the whiz kids could chew on. Another part of him, however, dwelt on what was disturbing him, working through its growing implications.

Oftentimes, Ziggy would come up with guesses she was 90, 95 percent certain were the job for this or that Leap, only to have Sam's intuition second-guess her and save the game at the last minute.

"Now from what we know or, well, from what we

theorize, anyway," Gushie continued, "the initial experiment that sent Dr. Beckett back—his consciousness, his soul, whatever—jumbled time. We've somehow got to get him back here into his own body again to cure that rift caused by that first Leap through the Accelerator."

But that's the problem, isn't it, Al asked himself. We can't seem to cure it. Every time Sam makes a correction, that correction doesn't seem to heal anything—it just sets another crack, or two or twenty-two, splitting off through time, and then Sam Leaps off again. Ziggy can't predict where fixing one crack is going to send Sam. All she can ever do is just guess at what correction has to be made once Sam gets there.

And *that* was what had Admiral Al Calavicci worried. It was the thing that he could not tell Tina or Gushie. The thing that he had never even told Sam. The thing known only to himself and to Ziggy.

They were affecting the present. When Sam made his corrections, things changed. Sometimes they changed a lot. Even Al did not know what all the changes were. In fact, whenever he went through the door to the past to help Sam—to bring him facts and information from Ziggy, to be his eyes and ears on the other side of the doors, or the world—he never knew what world he might be coming back to.

This was Al Calavicci's private burden. Most people, if they were forced to think about it, would have to admit they did not know for certain where their life was going from one day to the next. Anything, any little thing could happen and then suddenly—*bam*—their entire future

33

could be irreversibly changed. A wisp of past memory shot through Al's mind—a Ray Bradbury story in which rich time travelers were taken back millions of years to hunt dinosaurs. Those saurians selected as targets were picked moments before their deaths and no trophies were allowed to be taken home outside of photographs. The bodies were left to lie where they would have fallen anyway. The only thing the hunters had to do was stay on the trail provided by the time service people.

But, in the story, one hunter took a misstep and his foot went off the trail, killing a butterfly. That was all he did to time. He killed a butterfly. And yet, when the hunters returned to the future, they found their present completely changed . . . mostly for the worst.

What are we going to do? thought Al. This is serious. More serious than anything that's ever happened here. Ziggy is the only one who knows what the present was like before each of Sam's Leaps. She's the only one who remembers it all—who knows what's changed and what hasn't. And if she can't keep track . . .

Al shuddered, covering the involuntary response with a fake yawn that seemed to fool Gushie but not Tina.

What does it matter, thought Al. Any second now it could be Tina who's talking and Gushie will be the one who notices.

The admiral looked at the two technicians, thinking how different all their lives had been before, during, and after some Leaps. Once, he had left the Imaging Chamber knowing he had a date with Tina that night, only to come back from mid-Leap and find that Tina and Gushie were married. And that was just a change that had hap-

34

pened *inside* the Project. Who knew what was happening outside right now? The Soviets could still have nukes. They could be launching them. Elvis could be President. We might be sending manned missions to Mars, or half the country could be dying of some plague.

And, the thought hit him with horror, I wouldn't know it.

I wouldn't know because there's no Ziggy to tell me. There's no Ziggy to pinpoint where Sam is and to get me to him. We're helpless, more helpless than the first time Sam Leaped and we didn't have the faintest idea what was going on.

Al sighed to himself, trying to move his shoulders to indicate he was merely tired, not bored. Reaching for his coffee mug, he took another long pull, draining it as he thought, We're a lot more helpless this time. Because at least the first time we thought we might be able to get Sam back.

Setting his empty mug back down, Al focused his attention toward Gushie, thinking, At least then we still had hope.

CHAPTER
FIVE

As Sam was moving back in all of the things Betty had already packed in the station wagon, he found his wallet and keys on the mantelpiece over the fake fireplace. A quick inspection told him his last name, *Ralston,* and the year, *1986.* He also discovered he lived in Portland, Oregon, and that he owned an eighteen-wheeler that he used for long-distance hauling.

I wonder if I have any runs coming up, he thought. I wonder if this Leap might have something to do with that instead of Ralston's shaky relationship with his family? I hope not. I *think* I know how to drive a truck, but I'm not sure I want to risk my life on it.

Not wanting to spend too much time going through the wallet out in plain sight, Sam continued taking bags up to the second floor. Pulling another set out of the back of the car, he thought, Oh, well, maybe I'll Leap before Ward has to take anything anywhere.

Yeah, another Leap. There's something to look forward to.

Coward, he thought darkly.

Sam nearly dropped the bags. What, he wondered, could he have meant by that? Not wanting to guess, he returned to moving things into the house, trying to escape the sun before it made his head hurt even worse.

Inside, Betty left him to do the unpacking as she started lunch for everyone. While she worked at slicing bread and cold cuts, Sam worked at his own job. He was able to figure out where all of the bags containing clothing went easily enough. Everything else he simply piled in the upstairs hallway. He told Betty what he had done.

"I put the kids clothes in their rooms—yours back in ours. There were some other things . . ." Can't exactly tell her I don't know where anything goes—can I? "I just left them in the hall. I, well, I didn't want to . . . unpack them. I felt funny puttin' stuff back, without you there." Especially since I don't know where any of it goes.

Betty turned to look at him, a puzzled expression on her face.

"I'll help you put it all back later, if you want. But I have to admit, lunch seems like a good idea. I got a poundin' headache from last night. Coffee would hit the spot. Lots of black coffee." He grinned. "And then food. Did you and the kids eat yet? Before you started, ah, well . . . you know." Sam trailed off, looking at his feet as though they might have the answer to making this Leap easier.

"No," Betty admitted.

Turning away, she reached in the kitchen cabinet for a jar of mustard. There was still tension in the set of her shoulders, Sam noted.

The mustard jar was just out of her reach. Every time her nails reached it they would tap it a little farther away. Realizing what was happening, Sam moved across the kitchen without thinking, saying, "Here, honey, let me get that."

Betty moved aside, watching her husband fetch down the jar. She watched him closely. Sam carefully did not look at her to catch her reaction. Let her see that I'm not doing it to score points, he thought. Let her see I'm . . . just being helpful. Sam turned and handed her the jar. There were tears in her eyes.

Taking the jar from his hand, she managed to smile and say a pleasant "thank you."

As she turned away, returning to her work, Sam thought he heard her say, "Thank you, Lord."

"Can I do anything else?" he asked. "Slice some pickles or tomatoes?"

Betty was so clearly surprised at his offer that Sam almost had to apologize.

"I'm sorry. I guess I don't really help out very much around here, do I?"

"Oh, it's not that, Ward," she answered quickly. "It's just that . . . you know, this morning and all. I mean"— the woman clearly steeled herself to say the words— "we were walking out on you. We were leaving. And you, you're acting so different—you're acting—oh, God, please don't get upset, Ward, but you're—you're being so nice. Like nothing had happened—better than

38

if nothing had happened. Better than you, than . . . than in so long.''

"Guess if you thought you could change me so much by walking out you'd of done it a long time ago.''

Sam realized he had touched a nerve. As he spoke the words she must have been thinking, Betty lost control. Large, streaming tears burst out of her, followed by racking sobs.

He apologized again, but that only made her cry all the louder. Taking his host's wife into his arms, Sam shook his head wondering what kind of heel Ward Ralston truly was.

"Cry if you want to, or need to, but try and remember, sweetheart, I'm the one that was gettin' walked out on. *Nice* guys don't usually wake up to find their families loadin' up the station wagon for a one-way trip to Anywhere-else-ville.''

"Oh, God, Ward,'' cried Betty, hanging on fiercely to her husband. "What's happened to you? It's like it's too good to be true, like any minute you're just going to turn around and it's all going to stop.''

"It's all right, baby, it's all right. It's not going to stop,'' said Sam, wondering if he was making promises Ward would never keep. "I know it must seem different to you. Real different. Maybe even *too* different.''

Her tears slowing for a moment, Betty asked, "What—what do you mean?''

"I mean, well, last night I did more than get drunk,'' answered Sam. "I had a nightmare of some kind like I never had before. At first it was a good dream. Floatin' in the blue. But then it wasn't. I found myself fallin' instead of floatin'. And there was pain, like I was being shot with electricity, like I was on fire. It went on forever and it hurt so bad I couldn't think or breathe or anything.''

A part of Sam's brain warned him that he was coming dangerously close to telling Betty Ralston the truth, but he ignored it.

"I woke up and for a long time I was afraid to open my eyes. Honestly, sweetheart, I was afraid it would hurt me if I did. I was afraid I wouldn't know where I was, or who I was, or, or, or anything.''

Sam took Betty's head in his hands. It was done with tenderness, a thing Ward Ralston's hands could not do on their own without Sam's help.

Giving her the chance so many people beg the heavens for, but so few receive, he told her, "And I'm still not sure if I'm really me, or not. I mean, maybe God did somethin' to me. Maybe he did change me. Maybe you're goin' to have to put the pieces together for me. I mean, I'm holdin' your head, and my hands feel like they don't even understand how to do it without hurtin' you.''

Letting go of Betty, he lowered his arms down behind her back. Pulling her closer, he whispered, "I've been some kind of shit, and I don't even remember it. I know I've hurt you, and I know I've got a lot to make up for. And if you just tell me how, I will.''

Normally, Sam did not like to make promises for his hosts. Who knew if the people who came back to their bodies after he borrowed them lived up to the words he said, the deeds he left them with the credit for? Usually,

40

he tried to keep such things to a minimum. But the devastating pain of his last Leap had not been anything like any kind of usual he could remember.

And, he thought bitterly, if whoever's in charge of this ball game is going to change the rules that drastically, then so can I.

Hugging his wife—Ward's wife—even more closely to him, he told her, "Because all I know is only a fool would want to lose you, sweetheart."

Then he kissed her. It was a soft kiss at first, one Sam meant only to be reassuring. Instead, it grew into something much stronger. It ran longer and deeper than any kiss Sam had ever dared deliver in any Leap he could remember. In fact, the part of his mind detached enough to make comments told him it was the single longest kiss he had ever been involved in in his life. It was warm and rich and it tasted good. He was kissing someone who wanted to kiss him, who needed to kiss him, and for once he saw no reason to turn away.

Finally, though, Betty pulled away. Her face was glowing; smile as wide as it could be, eyes shining with a joy that Sam guessed had left them years before. What does she see? Sam thought.

Ward's hair still falls the same way, Ward's smile still curls up more to the left than the right, the scar on his forehead is still in the same place, his nose is still broken the same way—in both places. But can she see the same different *something* she had seen when he had first come downstairs that morning?

There *is* something different about me today, Betty,

he thought. Something awful different. I hope you like it.

Looking down at Betty, Sam smiled. At this moment, Leaping didn't seem important at all. He had a feeling that his life—Ward's life—was about to get better.

CHAPTER
SIX

"You know," said Al, not bothering to look at the folder in Tina's hand, "I'm getting mighty frustrated."

"You haven't even read the report," she protested.

Al merely rolled the unlit cigar in his mouth from one side to the other with his tongue, saying, "I read your face. Tell me there's anything in that folder I want to read."

"Okay," she said, dropping heavily into the chair next to him. "You win. We're still nowhere. No—correction. We're still ten steps out from nowhere."

"That," said Al, "is not the best news I've had today."

"Too bad. It's the best I've got to give. It's the best any of us has right now."

Tina opened the folder. Leaving the typed report inside, she pulled out a thick wad of transparencies. Once laid out on the table the stack of plastic sheets proved to be a multiple overlay schematic map of Ziggy's hardware systems.

Although the admiral was as interested in pouring over the computer's inner workings as he was bathing in running lava, he did his best to follow the engineer's verbal report on the team's progress. He poured himself another coffee and braced himself for the explanation. Try as he might, however, he could not keep his fatigued mind from wandering.

Oh, oh, my lovely Tina, he thought, staring at the beautiful redhead. Cara belle, Tina . . . Tina, Tina Martinez-O'Farrell. Tina Martinez-O'Farrell-Calavicci. Yes, that would be better. Tina Martinez-O'Farrell-Calavicci. One name from each of the major food groups.

Man, do I need some sleep.

Al laughed, not knowing what else to do. Hoping to distract himself, he stole a brief glance at his watch and then turned his attention back to Tina. Before he could focus on her, he realized he had not actually seen what time it was.

Hell, he thought, I can barely see Tina.

Looking at his watch again, he stared long and hard, trying to get the numbers on its face to come into focus. He could not. He had been awake, to the best of his knowledge, for two and a half days straight. Before that he had only been managing a few hours whenever he got the chance to catch some sleep in the first place.

"I apologize," said Al, putting his hand up suddenly to stop Tina's report. "I'm sorry to interrupt, but, ah''— he gave her a sheepish grin as he asked—''could you tell me what time it is?"

Tina smiled. She understood why Al might have to ask such a question after looking at his own watch.

"It's just about ten after eleven."

Al thanked her and was just ready to settle back in his chair when he realized he still didn't actually know what time it was. Even more sheepishly he interrupted the engineer a second time, apologized, and then asked her, "Which ten after eleven?"

"What?" asked Tina, puzzled.

"I meant A.M. or P.M.? I'm sorry," he explained. "I've been up so long, I don't know if it's day or night." He shrugged, gesturing helplessly as he added, "I've definitely lost track of the time . . ."

Al Calavicci started to laugh—not polite chuckles, but loud raucous noises that had him almost choking. Tina stared at him, watching the cigar fall from his lips. She watched as he slammed his open palm against the table. And then she watched as the hand's fingers curled into a fist, a fist that moved up and down, beating the tabletop over and over—hitting harder each time. After the first dozen hits, the engineer realized Al's laughter had turned into something else.

"Don't you get it?" he howled. "I lost track of the time! Hahahaha ha hahaaaa, ha ha—ha hahahaha—hah. I . . . lost . . . track . . . *of the time*!!"

Tina did not know what to make of what she was seeing. Machines she could deal with—inside and out. Men she knew how to handle—pretty much as thoroughly as she could machines. But this was not a man problem, this was a people problem. And people were

45

not one of Tina's specialties. Not by any stretch of the imagination.

"Al," she said, her voice shaky and tentative. "Are you okay?"

The admiral looked up. The harsh, black circles under his eyes seemed to swallow them, making his face look like a skull mask. The normally dapper Calavicci had not shaved, had not put on one of his painfully colorful ties, had not done anything except worry about the Project and his best friend for too many hours, and now his body had decided to claim retribution. He pointed toward the door, his hand shaking so hard Tina could barely see it clearly.

"Get out," he snarled suddenly. "Get out of here and get back down to Ziggy and make her all better!" Tina stayed frozen in her seat.

"Now, goddamnit!" he bellowed. His hand slammed the table again, harder. His hot mug tipped over. The plastic pages of Tina's schematic ruffled, coffee spilling across them. "Every second you're not down there working on that miserable tin monster is another second lost—changed—destroyed!"

Tina stood, nervous and off-balance. Like most truly beautiful women, she felt comfortable in one-on-one situations with men. But Al was not playing by the rules, and his behavior frightened the engineer, more than she would have thought possible.

"Calm down, Admiral," she said, grabbing for her charts and papers. "You're just tired."

"I'm tired?" growled Al, getting up out of his own seat. "You bet I'm tired. I'm tired of walking into the

Imaging Chamber and going through the door to Sam and not knowing what kind of world I'm going to come back to. I'm tired of having to ask for a breakdown from a machine as to who the President is, what the capital of South Dakota is, whether or not *Star Wars* got made.''

Tina did not know what Al was talking about.

To her, Al was suffering from overwork and nerves and stress, fear for his friend combined with a lack of sleep. As intelligent as she was, as brilliant as so many of the people connected to the Project were, there were none who could handle the idea that their present was not stable, but constantly shifting, an ever-changing, wildly moving thing of which no single piece at all was permanent. Some might be able to for a while, but sooner or later the metaphysical questions such an existence imposed would tear them apart.

Is this really my father, my sister, my uncle, daughter, wife, boyfriend, et cetera? Did I have this job yesterday? Was I rich this morning? Did I have this scar ten minutes ago? Will I still be fat tonight? Should I pay this parking ticket? Should I sort my plastics from my metals from my paper? Be faithful to my husband—feed my dog— finish my work—cut the grass—do the shopping?

Turning away from the frightened Tina, putting his back between them, Al tried to get a grip on himself.

What does it matter? What does anything matter? Why should you? Hell, why do anything you don't want to? Everything's going to disappear in a puff of smoke. Right?

Why should *anyone* do anything they don't want to anymore? Why should they pay their taxes? Or obey the speed limit? Why obey any laws? Why not do whatever we want—kill the creeps who give us bad service, cut us off in traffic, tell us we can't take something of theirs we like? That we want. Who is anyone to say no to me? To self-important me?

Al Calavicci had held himself in check since the beginning of Sam's Leaps only because of the special connection he shared with Sam and Ziggy. With part of their DNA built into the computer, Sam's allowing him to Leap, Al's allowing him to observe, they were tied into Ziggy's unique position in time and space. Ziggy existed, Sam Beckett existed, and so Al Calavicci existed. By concentrating on the fact that *he* was grounded in time, Al had remained immune to the terrors. He could barely imagine the levels of panic that might be reached if everyone knew how unstable all of time was in danger of becoming.

And now, he thought, you can't be smug anymore, can you, Calavicci? Ziggy's down for the count, and suddenly you're not privy to the inside track. Suddenly you don't know what's going to happen next, or what exactly happened yesterday, for that matter. You're as much at risk of disappearing without a trace as the next guy.

And you can't explain any of that to the person you just screamed your head off at.

Shaking his head, trying to clear the cobwebs away, Al turned back around.

"I'm sorry," he said to Gushie. "I could make the excuse that I've been up too long and that I'm just on edge, but that's not good enough. I'm getting crazy over all this, and a good sailor's supposed to know when he's working too hard and working everyone else too hard.''

"That's okay," answered the programmer, sticking out his hand. "I'm sorry we're not doing any better than we are. But with Tina out with the flu . . . you know . . ."

Al took the programmer's hand and shook it. With a wry smile, Al told Gushie that unfortunately for him, Gushie was too important awake and that sleep was out of the question until Ziggy was back on-line.

Gushie gave the admiral a quick "hah" and then gathered up the presentation folder he had brought to their meeting.

As Al busied himself unwrapping his cigar, Dr. Beeks told him, "That's why I told Gushie and Tina to stay right where they were and to keep working. What's the sense of either of them coming up here to tell you in fancy terms what you already know, that Ziggy's not working?"

"That's what I tried to tell them, too," he said, grateful for having been able to avoid such a senseless meeting.

"I also told them I was ordering you to bed," said the doctor, her arms folded across her chest. "And I am, too, before you fall apart. You look terrible, you know."

"Yeah," agreed Al, unable to stifle a yawn.

Damn, he thought, staring hard at his watch, trying to make out the time, I must really need some sleep.

Standing, he stretched his arms to their full length, picked up his hot mug full of coffee, and then headed for the door, talking to himself in a dry, tired voice, "I don't know why I bother to schedule meetings when no one's going to show up."

49

CHAPTER
SEVEN

Sam woke up slowly, cautiously, wondering what his last Leap could have been about.

"Oh, boy," he groaned, not knowing where he was. Or when. Or why. "That was *not* a good Leap."

He had, of course, scanned the room to see if he was alone before he had spoken. Certain he was, he sat up, not quite ready to get out of bed. It felt too comfortable, too peaceful, and it was not a luxury that most Leaps afforded him.

No, most of the time I'm in a jail cell getting my head thumped, or being knocked around by my own mother, or . . . Suddenly Sam dropped the line of thought, remembering the pain and turmoil of the Leap he had just been through.

Well, yes. What caused that, anyway? I don't think I've ever had a Leap like that . . . ever. Even with the Swiss-cheesing, I think I'd remember something like that if it had ever happened before.

Up until now, all of his Leaps had been beautiful things. To him, there was always the same shimmering light that would come down and wash over and envelop him after he had completed whatever his latest task was. Then he would find himself floating—somewhere—lost in blue-white light.

To Sam Beckett there were no recordable sensations—no feeling of weight, no scents or tastes—nothing to see or hear—nothing but the surrounding light. If he was moving—racing along through the void at a billion miles a second or hanging stock-still in the same point every single time—he had no way of knowing.

At times he thought of it as his personal holding area. Sometimes he simply called it Limbo or the Ether. What and where it was did not matter, however.

I can study it when the Leaping is over. Whenever I get back home.

Whenever he Leaped into a new body, into whatever new circumstance he was supposed to patch up, two things always happened sooner or later. First he thought about getting back home, about being back at the Project—being able to sit back and look at his experiences, to evaluate what had happened to him without having to do it anymore . . . at least, until he stepped into the Accelerator again.

And you would, too, wouldn't you? He almost laughed. After all we've been through, you'd do it—again . . . you'd step up there and go ahead and do it all over again.

Secondly, no matter how he tried to quiet it, a part of

51

him would protest his Leaping—would demand he try and stop the process, by whatever means necessary.

This time that part was missing.

Dr. Sam Beckett, the analytical thinker, the Nobel prizewinner with six or seven widely variant degrees under his belt, was not the kind of man to let such a change in his habits slip by unnoticed. Now, lying in bed, he was forced to wonder if the power that had trapped him within the continuum of time had done something to him . . . something to change his outlook, to make him more . . .

More what? Pliable? Receptive? What?

"You, Dr. Beckett," he said in a whisper, staring at the ceiling, brow furrowed in thought, "are lying here being paranoid when you should be finding out who you are." Looking around, he saw a large, richly appointed room filled with handsome, dark wood furniture.

"Well, whoever you are, you look like you're doing all right for yourself."

Getting out of bed, he started a search of the bedroom, looking for the usual clues. While he rifled through his newest host's belongings, his subconscious began ordering the facts he had over his latest question so he could review them later. Why had he experienced such a bad Leap? What could have caused such a fundamentally different experience? And where was his indignation, his outrage, over being used like a repairman forced to make house calls?

Looking at his new self in the mirror, he took in what he had to work with this time.

Male, Caucasian, six-two, three, maybe. Blue-gray

eyes, strong chin, good shoulders, back—he took a glance down—legs, everything. Not bad. Nice to be . . . closer to the original model for once.

The next drawer opened brought him underwear and socks. Shedding the briefs his host used for sleeping, he pulled on a set of each and turned to the chair near the dresser where a pair of pants lay hooked over the back. He got into those next, pleased to find a wallet inside.

All right, he thought, reading bits and pieces from the cards he had pulled from the wallet as he buttoned up the shirt he had taken from another drawer, let's see here. The year is 1986, and you, Mark Ralston, appear to be thirty-nine or forty years old—depending on the month, living in Reno, Nevada, on the faculty of the University of Nevada. You are blessed with a driver's license, type AB negative blood with a rare RH factor to boot, membership in the Audubon Society and the Sierra Club, and all the major credit cards.

Sam studied himself in the mirror again, wondering if Mark Ralston was the sort to appear in public without a tie. He wondered for only a moment. His host did not keep an easily accessible selection of ties available. The majority of his shirts were not the type that matched the few ties he did have.

Besides, for all I know it's Saturday and I'm supposed to be white-water rafting somewhere.

Brushing his hair with his hands, he found it swept easily into place and stayed there. Moving back to the chair that served as the man of the house's valet, he slipped into the shoes that were stored under it neatly. He stood up and noticed two impressions worn in the carpeting that told him that shoes—the ones he had on and probably quite a few pair before them—had been kept precisely there for years.

"So," Sam asked the black-haired man staring at him from the mirror, "what's your problem, Professor? You're young, good-looking, and well enough off that the world should be your oyster." Changing his accent to a giddy Irish brogue, giving the face in the mirror an imaginary tip-of-the-hat, he added, "But you wouldn't have called for our services if things were all peaches and cream, now would ya, sir?"

Sam smiled, gave himself a short salute, and then turned for the door. Another thing was wrong, he thought suddenly. Al was overdue. If he had actually been asleep, Al was hours overdue. That was unusual.

Maybe he came and just couldn't wake me up. Sam thought as he left the bedroom. The rest of the large apartment was dressed with deep carpeting and the same lush, expensive sensibilities as the bedroom. Spotting a standing covered cup, he crossed the room and picked it up, whistling low as he examined it.

German, eighteenth century, mother-of-pearl and horn with silver-gilt mounts. Topped with a carved lamb with a silver collar.

"My God, Professor Ralston," he said aloud as he replaced the cup on its stand, "you like beautiful things, don't you?"

Moving across to the doctor's display shelves, Sam racked his brain trying to place the pieces he was seeing. Teapots and jardinieres looking to be made of Viennese porcelain, a box in the form of a chambered nautilus so

54

unusual, with such care and attention given to its work, that Sam wondered if it was Nymphenberg work.

He could not remember how it was he knew about German antiques. He could not dredge up any memories of his life before his first Leap that gave him any particular knowledge in that area. Nor could he remember any Leaps where he might have picked up such details. But he knew what he was looking at.

What did it matter, he thought, how he knew? Maybe his host was passing along information, some kind of left-behind memory. That had happened before—hadn't it? Maybe he had an aunt who loved German antiques when he was a boy that he just could not remember at that moment. All of that was unimportant.

"What is important is getting down to work and finding out what this guy's problem is . . . getting it solved and getting on to the next Leap."

Sam smiled. For once he didn't feel overwhelmed by the need to get back to Albuquerque. Finally, he was ready to throw all of his energy into his Leaps, with no part of him tired of the process, with no part of him wishing for the Leaps to end.

It was a relief, in a way.

CHAPTER
EIGHT

Al could not believe it. He had finally gotten some sleep—actually more than an hour. In fact, as best he could tell, it had been a full four and three-quarters hours. True, it had been on a chair, but it had been sleep. He could remember sitting down to catch his breath before he pulled his socks off, a memory that in itself made him grimace.

God, Calavicci, you're getting so old you have to sit down to take off your socks.

The admiral preferred to stand on one leg to take off and put on his socks. He was an old Navy man, and even old Navy men who spent more of their career time in jets and space capsules . . . or VC prison camps . . . than on board ship liked to pride themselves on being able to do anything on their feet. Rolling decks were a challenge to master, and sailors liked to be able to brag they could do anything—absolutely anything—at any time of the day or night on the worst seas ever experienced by man.

Al stirred himself and pushed up out of the chair, remembering a particular moment of astronaut training. It was one of the more strenuous zero-gravity experiments—eating. Suddenly he saw himself as he was then, with another Navy man, Benjamin Higgens.

The memory came to him clearly—the two of them standing outside the KC130 the Air Force used for simulation testing. The big modified 707 would be taken to almost forty thousand feet and then the pilot would go into an elliptical dive, giving the trainees twenty to forty seconds of free-fall experience. The testing room had been padded from top to bottom to protect the ribs and skulls of the astronauts.

Higgens was one of the toughest men Al had ever known. He could take more punishment than any two other men, and he knew it. After he saw the padding, Higgens had made more than one comment on how fragile flyboys must be. The Air Force officers in charge of testing had let him quip, knowing full well how things were going to turn out. Then Higgens had laughed at the tubes of food paste and the cups with built-in straws and pressure seals they would be using. He had boldly announced, much to Al's chagrin, that such toys might be needed by the Air Force, but that he and Al could eat a full Norman Rockwell Thanksgiving dinner in zero gravity without missing a pea.

Oh, the admiral remembered, the Higg had been most spit and polish all the way—but he just had to take the interdepartmental dig at the observing officers.

"Why, yes, sir," he had told them, fighting to keep his thousand-kilowatt smile in check. "Any two gobs who can dunk sinkers and not spill a drop of coffee all night on the open watch deck of an escort bobber during a class eight typhoon can certainly handle this."

Stripping off his clothes he had slept in, Al remembered their instructor trying hard to suppress a smile as he took the Higg at his word. The instructor had had a pot of coffee, a carton of cream, a score of sugar cubes, and a dozen doughnuts brought to the zero-gravity chamber. Then he had ordered the pair to go inside and not come out until they had finished every drop and crumb.

Heading into the shower, the admiral remembered the hours it had taken them during dive after dive, chasing floating pieces of cake around the room, sucking flying lines of coffee out of the air, licking up drops of cream off the ceiling. They had put on quite a show, and their apology to the Air Force had been most humble. But it was one of Al's fondest memories from the program.

And now, he thought, almost sadly, I'm falling asleep in chairs.

Washing away a number of layers of sweat and grime, the admiral started to plan out his next moves. Ideally, he would have liked to just turn around and get into the bed he had been headed for roughly five hours earlier. But the only reason he was awake in the first place was because of a message from Dr. Beeks asking him to meet her in the Waiting Room.

There had been nothing particularly urgent to the wording of the note delivered to him. Nor was Al one

58

to jump to conclusions. But for a minor staffer to knock on his door for almost ten minutes until Al dragged himself out of dreamland meant she had been told not to come back without having both found the admiral and delivered the doctor's message.

Stepping out of the shower, Al was amazed at how much better he felt than before he had crashed. The cramps that had knotted his arms and back had faded. He had still been a bit stiff when he had entered the shower, but after fifteen minutes under the hot water—ten of them just relaxing under the massage head and breathing steam—he was beginning to feel as if he could handle anything.

That's good, Al, came one of his nagging voices, because unless God came down and tapped Ziggy on her imaginary head and said "Arise," you're still in charge of a multibillion-dollar mess.

Throwing his towel on his bed, Al crossed the room to his closet. Sliding it open, he looked for just the right outfit in which to confront Dr. Beeks.

Oh, yeah, Calavicci . . . you've got you're best friend lost out in the ozone somewhere, and you've got no supercomputer to get you to him anymore. Your technicians don't seem to be able to get it going, and you've got no ideas, either. Sam is probably going nuts wondering where you are, and why not? You're only what? Days late by now? No big deal. You just keep playing peacock . . . Sam can wait, right?

Pulling out a double-breasted, blue pinstripe, Al threw it on the bed next to his towel while he told his conscience, "Listen, Beeks has got some kind of a problem

59

and that most likely means *Sam* has another problem besides not hearing from us.''

Finding the shirt he was after, Al pulled it out and then went after his fluorescent purple tie, the one with the tiny bright pink squares and circles he had been given just before he had retired.

"So, Tina and Gushie will just have to fix Ziggy without me. I do have this whole place to run—remember?" Grumbling, he rounded up the rest of what he would need to put on to be able to go out into the Project.

Great, I'm sitting down to put on my socks *and* I'm talking to myself. And all in one day.

Al walked into the Waiting Room twelve minutes later. He had purposely left his hot mug in his quarters. For the moment he was feeling awake and even alert. He would switch back to coffee whenever the good effects produced by the sleep he had managed to get began to wear off.

Verbeena Beeks met him at the door. The look etched into her ebony features did not bode well. Before either of them said anything, Al snuck a quick peek in the direction of Sam's body.

Everything *looks* squared away, he thought. So, what else is wrong around here that I can't do anything about?

"Okay, Verbeena. Spill it. What's the problem?"

Stepping aside so that the admiral could see Dr. Beckett's physical shell more clearly, she said, "You tell me."

Al moved forward, trying to figure out what the new problem was. The body in the bed before him did not move. It was alive, the chest rose and fell, nostrils expanded and contracted. He saw the eyes blink, even caught a little motor action in the fingers and toes. But, outside of that, nothing. Sam's eyes were open—his body was not asleep. But it was not doing anything else, either.

"Okay," said Al. "You got me here, I'm all yours. I'll ask it again—what's the problem? I mean, usually whoever comes through the Leap and ends up in Sam is either crying or screaming or demanding to go home or telling us we're just a dream. You either have to drug them or have them restrained."

Walking around the bed situated in the middle of the Waiting Room, Al paid scant attention to the monitors attached to Sam's body. They told him little. Watching and interpreting them was the doctor's job. Al knew how to delegate authority. The Navy taught its officers that in their first ten minutes. But Beeks was a civilian and, for that matter, so was he now. And so he ended up playing the kinds of games people with no clear power structure played.

"This should be a picnic. Whoever's in there isn't ranting, making demands, throwing food—nothing." Growing a trifle annoyed, Al said, "I've got a bigger problem right now if you don't mind. Ziggy can't find Sam. Hell, I don't think Ziggy can do basic subtraction right now. What do you want from me, Verbeena? For God's sake—you've got it easy for once. You haven't even got . . ."

Then it hit Al. All at once. Like a mule.

"Oh . . . no . . ."

Gripping the side of the bed, the admiral stared into Sam Beckett's eyes, finally understanding the enormity of the doctor's concern.

"You beginning to get the idea, Admiral?"

"He hasn't said anything? He hasn't moved?" The doctor shook her head. "Not at all? In the entire time since the last Leap?" The doctor shook her head again. "There hasn't been anything? No words, no movements, nothing?" The doctor continued shaking her head until Al ran out of different ways to ask the same two questions.

Finally, he asked, "Has this ever happened before?" Again she shook her head. "Nothing like it, ever?" Tired of making the same motion, the woman merely locked her eyes on Al's. Giving in, the admiral asked, "What's it mean?"

"I don't know. But you are in charge around here. You had to be made aware of the situation."

"That's it?" asked Al, stunned. He stared at the unmoving body on the bed, then asked again, "That's it? That's all you can come up with?"

"Yes, Admiral. That's all I have. You're not the only one living on coffee and IOUs right now."

"Maybe," said Al, snapping his fingers, "maybe this is why Ziggy can't pinpoint Sam. Maybe it's because he isn't lost anymore. Maybe he's Leaped back and, and . . . and he's just in some kind of shock or something."

"Thought of it," answered the doctor. "I asked Tina and Gushie. They didn't think Sam Leaping back would cause Ziggy to break down." She sighed. "I tried a battery of stimulants. Nothing worked. And before you jump to the other end of the wild conclusion spectrum, let me save you the trouble.''

Taking a deep breath, Dr. Beeks shot it out in a fierce exhale and then took another, saying, ''No, I don't think Sam's dead. I've run enough tests on his body to convince me that someone is in there. Someone's spirit or mind, or whatever you want to call it. That,'' she said, pointing at Sam Beckett's body, ''is not a vegetable.''

''You're saying what?'' asked Al, hopefully. ''That he's got brain activity?''

''All he needs and then some. There's enough going on inside his head right now for two people. So, no, the answer is not that Sam is back to stay or gone for good. Whatever is really going on is somewhere in the middle.''

Yeah, thought Al, ain't it always?

He turned back to Sam's body, staring at it, searching for some clue there in the Waiting Room that might somehow explain the problems in the Imaging Chamber. There was no doubt that the two problems were related. It was impossible to have two things so far outside of their normal routine happen at the same time not to be somehow connected.

Al laughed at that.

Outside our normal routine? Our *normal routine*? And would you kindly tell the rest of the class what it is you consider to be *our normal routine*?

Backing away from Sam's body, Al took the doctor's arm gently.

''Watch him. Watch over him. Obviously if you don't

have any answers, neither do I. There's something going on here, Verbeena. Something bad and it's got me scared."

Dr. Beeks stared at Al. As a psychiatrist she was used to people making startling statements. Thus she did not register her shock that Al Calavicci could admit to anyone that anything could scare him. But it did shock her. Not because she didn't believe he could be scared; he was human, just like the rest of them. But to admit it to *her*, the Project shrink, and not even realize it—that spooked her.

Backing toward the door, his eyes locked on the still unmoving body, Al said, "You keep me posted. If anything—anything happens, you get me ASAP. In the meantime . . . talk to him."

"I have been . . ."

"I didn't ask for a list, Doctor," barked the admiral, tired of civilian games. Shifting his gaze to Beeks, he said fiercely, "I said talk to him. Ask him, or her—whatever—questions. Twenty thousand of them if you have to. Whoever's in there, get them out here with us. Hell, pour coffee down his throat if that's what it takes to wake him up!"

He looked once more at the figure on the bed, turned, and walked out the door, muttering under his breath.

"Before we can't."

Walking to the Control Room, Al stripped off his tie, stuffing it into his jacket. Then, pulling his jacket off as well, he hung it over his left arm and started unbuttoning buttons. First the one at his collar, then the one at his right wrist. Getting his left cuff open, he began rolling up his sleeves.

"You hang on, pal, because we're coming for you. Oh, yeah," he promised, "we're coming for you all right, and this time . . ." He pulled open the door to the Control Room, words growling within his throat, "This time we're going to get you back."

CHAPTER

NINE

It had not taken Sam all that long to get Ward's eighteen-wheeler moving.

Oh, we've got it moving, all right, he thought desperately as he tore down the freeway clocking nearly eighty miles an hour. Now if we can just keep it moving in the right direction, and not move it *over* someone, maybe we'll be okay.

Still, it gave him a certain sense of accomplishment to be able to put the big rig through its paces without stripping its gears, let alone without turning it over and killing Ward Ralston and maybe himself. Now, all he had to do was make Ward's string of runs. Sam went over the itinerary in his head.

First, he had to get the truckload of spring bearings he had picked up in Medord, Oregon, all the way down to Boulder City in Nevada. Which meant cutting through the desert to Las Vegas.

Be nice to see Vegas. He hadn't been there since a conference in . . . what year was it? Sam thought for a few minutes, then gave up. It had been a while, and he hadn't seen much of the city then, just the hotel the conference was in. He'd make sure to see the sights *this* time.

Then it was just a hop over the border into Arizona to grab a load of chair legs sitting in a warehouse in Kingman that had to be delivered to a manufacturing house in Elko.

Elko.

The word echoed in Sam's brain, as if he was less than impressed with the town. Again, he was picking up traces of his host—had to be. As far as he knew, Sam Beckett had never been in Elko, much less developed an opinion about it one way or the other.

I wonder why Ward doesn't like Elko? Sam thought uneasily. He'd find out soon enough, he supposed.

The furniture maker in Elko had a piecemeal job he wanted Ward to take on with him, four different shipments he was sure would fit in one load. Sam would have to stop in Winnemucca and Sparks, which were both on 80, but then dip down to Carson City and on to Lake Tahoe. It would mean unloading almost the entire truck at each stop, but slow-downs like that just jacked his price up.

Ward had not planned time to celebrate the run in his itinerary, though. According to his notes, there was another, much more important delivery to make when this one was done. One that would apparently pay him much more.

67

Things could be worse for you, Ward ol' boy, Sam thought. Things could be worse.

Sam looked around the cab, trying to add some dimension to the profile of Ward Ralston he had built in his head. As bad as some of the evidence was against his current host, he found himself liking certain things about him.

They were all little things—his taste in music, his taste in coffee, hot and strong, the way he kept the rows of his garden straight, the orderly business records he kept . . .

None of that, of course, made up for Ward's actions toward his family, but it made Sam feel that maybe there was something positive about his host, something Sam Beckett could work with.

"And do what?" a small voice asked him.

Good question, Sam thought, watching the desert zip past the windows on both sides. So far, I've gotten the first load on board, and I think I've figured out what I'm supposed to be doing. Now I've got three days on the road before I go back and run right out again on Wade's mystery run. Which means that I'm going to be at this for a week before I ever get to concentrate on why I'm actually here—Betty and the kids.

Sam scanned the horizon absently, checking for the possibility of police. Catching himself, he slapped the steering wheel in disgust.

"Great, I earn six advanced degrees so I can finally settle down into the life of a truck driver."

Oh, feeling a bit of the snob today, are we, Sam? Feeling a little too high and mighty to be Ward Ralston for a week?

"No, it's not that," he said aloud, his eyes moving from windshield to mirror to mirror. "If I'm on the road, how am I supposed to work on why I'm really here?"

But, of course, the problem was, Sam was just assuming that he was here to patch up Ward's family life. Making Ward's runs might be exactly what was needed to do that. And there was no guarantee he was there to fix Ward's life, anyway. Maybe he saved the furniture manufacturer from ruin by making his run on time, which Ward might not have. Who knew?

"Not me," muttered Sam. "Not without any information." Ramming the gas pedal to the floor, Sam ran through the gears just for practice, to bleed off a little of his frustration, shouting at the top of his lungs, "Where are you, Al? Where the hell are you anyway?! What's going on? Why aren't you here? How am I supposed to know what to do?"

If his situation had been fictional, of course, that would have been the moment Al arrived. A dramatic outburst and then—ta da—in would come the garishly dressed cavalry, bringing the much-needed answers. But Dr. Sam Beckett, no matter how much his life might have appeared like science fiction to someone else, was trapped in a seemingly never-ending cycle of . . .

"Of what?!" he asked—demanded. "Will someone simply just please tell me that?" He was tired, suddenly. Tired of being the eternal Nice Guy, always Leaping in to fix what some other schmuck had fouled up. Unlike some Leaps, where he could almost *feel* the importance of what he was doing, this time seemed pointless, petty.

"Why should I care, anyway? Would Ward Ralston do this for me?"

As he said the word "this," Sam spread his hands away from the steering wheel for a moment, using them to indicate the cab of the eighteen-wheeler.

"Who's deciding all of this? Who picks and chooses these people? And why? For God's sake . . . why?"

With that rewording, the question changed. No longer was he simply questioning his current Leap, but the very process of Leaping itself. Sam stared out through the windshield, following the line of the road leading him away from Reno and down toward Boulder City.

It was a straight line, a long thin ribbon that did not curve out of sight but simply disappeared through contraction. Although he knew that it continued past the horizon, his eyes could not perceive its end. Instead they fed his brain the information that the road was narrowing until at last it folded in on itself. It was an illusion, of course, but one so vast that although he had the intelligence to understand it, he could not see through or dispel it.

A lot like Leaping, he thought bitterly. Except even I don't have the intelligence to understand Leaping . . . let alone make it go away.

"Even you?" The voice had a mocking tone, one he was sure came from outside him. Not a person calling to him, or the radio, or any other mundane source, but a voice which he had heard only once before, during a Leap. It frightened him, badly.

Looking about the cab as if he were going to find

Something floating in one of its corners, he began making his way off the road, afraid he was about to Leap. Or worse.

He certainly didn't want to leave Ward's body while he was traveling down the road at high speed. Would Ward just slip in and take over as if he had been there all along? Sam didn't know. He had no idea how his hosts reacted when they returned, and in this case it was too great a risk.

Easing the large rig off to the side of the road, Sam shut the engine off and sank his head onto the steering wheel, trying to regain his equilibrium. Sweat from more than the desert heat dampened his brow and neck, and he reached for a bandanna to wipe it away. Suddenly it was too stuffy in the cab. Throwing open the passenger side door, Sam jumped down to the ground.

His boots dug into the dried-out soil and sand, crushing the brittle remains of a long dead bush. Brown and gray leaves broke free, catching in the hot breeze and floating away. Splinters clung to Sam's boots and jeans, bits coming free and falling across the desert floor with each step he took.

There was a pain bubbling within him, one that reached from his skull down into his chest and lower. It tightened around his heart and lungs, making it hard to breathe, hard to move.

"What?" he cried out, worn beyond patience by the game Fate seemed intent on playing with him. "What do you want me to do? What do you want me to do now?"

Turning away from the truck, he stared out into the

71

desert. The landscape was rutted with the memory of long-gone streams and storms. Scrub brush broke the surface in a thousand spots—harsh, dry bushes barely green. Here and there large cactus trees twisted up out of the ground—more of them dead and disintegrating than alive. There were mountains in the distance as well, but like everything else Sam saw, they held no answers.

"What did I do?" he yelled to the uncaring desert. "Would someone please tell me what I did to deserve this?"

He stared up into the bright noon sky. It was broken only in a few places by thin patches of slow-moving clouds. There was no answer there, either. The sun continued to beat fiercely, the superheated air around him drying his skin, choking his breath.

"Did I break some kind of cosmic rules? What happened? Did we go too far? Pasteurization, neurosurgery, crop rotation—that was all right. Split the atom, that was okay. I guess leaving the planet was fine, too—right? Right? You didn't punish anyone for walking on the moon—not that we know of, anyway. But me . . . I went too far—right? *Right?!*"

Sam knew that he was overreacting, but couldn't seem to stop himself. He felt an urge to throw himself on the ground and throw a temper tantrum but he controlled it—barely.

"Dr. Sam Beckett—he presumed too much," he continued, his voice heavy with sarcasm. "Muck around with time and suddenly you've stepped over the boundary. I guess I broke the rules of humanity's apprenticeship? Went too far, too fast, for someone."

72

Pulling himself together, Sam raised his head and stared off toward the horizon. As the sun continued to bake down on him, he whispered, "All right, maybe I did play with something without thinking—without giving it the reverence it deserved. Maybe I even sinned against nature. I never tried to say I wasn't a sinner. But . . . I didn't sin every day."

Looking up into the overhead sun, Sam said, "Why do you have to punish me . . . every day?"

Sam lowered his head, rubbing at his eyes. Flashes of white and pink and yellow danced in his field of vision. He shook his head gently, rubbing at his temples afterward. He had held his anger back for so long, afraid to question, afraid to rage against his fate.

No, not afraid. Always before there had been a debate within him, a part of him that wanted to Leap, that argued whenever he questioned the right or wrong of his situation. But now, that part of him was gone—that voice silent. So he had taken the chance and questioned the great beyond. And the great beyond had had nothing whatsoever to say to him.

Dusting himself off, Sam sucked down his emotions—his frustrations and his fear and his rage. He was Dr. Sam Beckett, and he was still in Ward Ralston's body. And that was all there was to it. He had done the best he could to change that situation, but so far, whatever it was he was supposed to be doing—he had not discovered it.

Turning on his heel, he started back for his truck, wondering what next. He had fixed Ward's marriage, turned it around on the day his wife was walking out the door, but no, that was not enough. He had gone after the kids then, thinking they might be the problem.

When Taylor had disappeared before lunch, Sam had spent nearly six hours walking all over the neighborhood, into town and back, looking for him. He finally found the boy at home. Taylor had taken him on a goose chase that led back to his own room. He had done it to provoke Ward, to get the beating he needed to prove what his father was, to his mother, to himself. He had not gotten it. Sam had talked with him, cajoled him, done the father/son, man-to-man, buddy/pal number with him. And it had worked.

Seeing her mother happy and her brother reassured was all that Barbara had needed. In less than half a day, Sam had given Ward's entire family back the lives they thought they had lost. But that had not been enough, either. Sam did not Leap.

I could have let them go and it wouldn't have mattered, thought Sam as he continued to walk back to his truck.

Right? he questioned the unknown. Right? They might as well be halfway to her mother's or wherever they were going, for all you care.

Coming up alongside his rig, Sam stopped, turning back to look out into the desert. Staring at the far horizon, he said, ''I beg you for guidance every time I turn around, and the only time you make a sound is to tell me I'm too arrogant. Well, I've got news for you. I'm not the only one who's arrogant.''

Climbing back up into the cab, Sam thought back to the first time he had been bathed in the blue-white

74

light—the first time he had hung in the unexplainable part of the cosmos through which he Leaped. The voice that had spoken to him, the same voice he had heard again today, had surrounded him as the light had surrounded him. They had been around him and yet a part of him, the voice and the light both. In fact, he had often wondered just how much of them had been him.

Pulling the door shut behind him, Sam thudded down onto the seat and then slid over behind the steering wheel. Putting his hands on it, he ran his fingers around its circumference. Metaphysics might be good for the soul, he thought, but this, this I can touch. This, at least, is real.

Gunning the motor, he shouted over it, "You want arrogance—I'll give you arrogance. I don't think there is any great controlling force. I think I'm on my own here and that if I keep Leaping for another ten thousand years that's all that'll happen . . . I'll just keep Leaping." Pulling off the shoulder, Sam started running through the gears.

"Well, you lose this time. Betty's a great woman, and she's got two great kids. And guess what . . . she's got me, now, too." As the massive rig's speed started to climb, Sam filled the air with the sound of the air horns, screaming over them, "You understand? I'm not leaving this time! I'm staying. Find yourself another errand boy. I give up. I quit. Ward Ralston didn't deserve this life—but I do! I deserve it . . . and I'm taking it. Do you hear me? *I'm taking it!!*"

CHAPTER
TEN

"Well," mumbled Sam to himself, "if someone can find me a problem to fix in this guy's life, I'll be happy to get to work on it."

"Excuse me, Professor Ralston," asked a shorter, balding man, one of the group walking alongside of Sam. "I'm afraid I didn't catch that last."

"Oh, nothing, nothing, Dr. Klein," Sam answered, picking up the last thread of the conversation he had been taking part in and running with it. Sighing inwardly as the debate raged around him, he thought, Now this feels familiar.

When he was a child—teenager—he had always regarded his photographic memory as a curse. It had always given him every answer, every bit of the past— every page he had ever seen, note he had ever heard— instantly, and others had resented him for it. Now during his Leaps, even though vast parts of his memory were oftentimes sheared away, his ability to memorize seemed to always stay with him.

No matter whose life he sprang into, whatever the facts of it were, he learned them as he went along and remembered them during his entire stay.

Good thing, too, Sam thought. Professor Ralston has got a lot of life to keep straight.

He had been in his new host for several days, and so far it had been a daunting challenge for him to keep up with the man's schedule. It was not that the professor could challenge Sam academically. Sam was still the one with the IQ of a certified genius, multiple doctorates, fluency in seven modern languages and four dead ones. But the professor was an intellectual, active man.

Even though he was the head of the university's psychology department, he still taught a full class load. In a time where most schools only required their junior professors to take on such workloads, such dedication was an eyebrow-raiser. But that was not all he did. His student open-door hours were set as strictly as the rest of the staff, but it was well known that anytime he was in his office he was fair game for anyone who might wander in.

He also found the time to publish more papers and articles than anyone else within his department. And he logged an incredible number of lab hours, contributing to the university's research prestige. It seemed he was particularly noted for spending more time helping other people tweak their research without seeking credit than he did on his own.

In what copious spare time he had left over, Professor

Ralston somehow managed to keep his hand in as an antique collector and as an environmental activist. And he was apparently in the middle of writing two books at the same time.

Plus the ladies find Professor Ralston irresistible, too, thought Sam, remembering a phone message from a young woman named Anna. So would someone tell me just what it is that needs fixing around here?

Sam had to admit that he was growing increasingly perplexed. Ralston was, from all appearances, a happy, healthy bachelor with a full life and plenty of friends. He had no ex-wives Sam could find any trace of, no children lurking in the background, or at least none that the professor's apartment or office spoke of through wall-hung or desk-mounted pictures, photo albums, divorce papers, court orders, birth certificates, et cetera. So far, the only problem in Ralston's life came when he ran out of coffee, and everyone in his department was trained to prevent that. If there were any hidden scandals brewing somewhere that the professor was about to sink into, Sam could not find any trace of them. And if there was something amiss with one of his students, or a colleague, it was certainly not obvious.

Anyway, long-range impending disasters generally weren't the way things worked. When he Leaped, he always came in close to the middle of things. He had never gotten any length preparation time before.

Now, I seem to have all the time in the world. And Al's not here. And I should be scared. But mostly—I'm curious.

"Okay, Ralston," said Klein, playing the obvious devil's advocate, "Carstairs has thrown the gauntlet. Are you going to pick it up or not?"

Sam had been listening with one track of his mind, letting a second level ponder the problems of Dr. Beckett while the first paid attention to the concerns of Professor Ralston. Shifting his full faculties to the front for the moment, he chuckled briefly as a dodge to gain a moment, then said, "Well, Carstairs has indeed made his point—a point once made equally well with half the facts and twice the bluster by Jung. It is also a point I refuted in my last book . . . on page 438, if I remember correctly."

Those around him laughed, waiting for Carstairs to begin his attack anew, as the quintet of psychology professors made their way across the parking lot toward the lecture hall. The friendly argument continued, Klein and the others mostly taking a back seat to Carstairs and Sam. It was a good-natured contest—the kind of fine-tuned bickering in which most academic types loved to indulge.

Beneath that, however, Sam continued to wonder. Where was Al? What was keeping him? Did it have something to do with his bad Leap? That much seemed obvious.

First the Leap from hell. I miss the blue lights and the angel trumpets and get batted around by the celestial version of the Dallas Cowboys. Wrong thing number one.

Gazing at his watch, Sam noted that they would be on time for the lecture they were all attending. Smiling as Carstairs made a valid point Sam privately agreed with, but which he knew Ralston would not, he began backing up the professor's viewpoint while he thought, Then I land in a life that just doesn't seem to need any fixing. Our Professor Ralston is highly educated, respected, financially well off, good-looking, and popular. No bad debts, no enemies, not living in the center of some historic maelstrom—nothing. Wrong thing number two.

Klein beat his palm against Ralston's shoulder, laughing and guffawing in response to Carstairs's rebuttal. Sam smiled himself. He had to respect the much younger professor for keeping with the debate. Could he be the reason Sam was here? Carstairs had a lot going for him, including the fact that Sam knew he was on the right track with some of his theories.

He could not tell him so directly without creating more trouble in time, however, so he settled for giving him a smile that tried to convey that Ralston was actually thinking about what the younger man had to say rather than just dismissing it. In fact, Sam went so far as to say, "Well, you know, when you put it that way, Carstairs, that last point of yours might just actually be something to think about."

"Uh-oh," said one of the others in a kidding voice. "Watch him close now, Carstairs. He *does* have two books under deadline right now."

"Soooo," crowed one of the others, an older man by the name of Frellinberg, an exaggerated look of false surprise on his face, "*that's* how you keep your publishing schedule so far ahead of the rest of us, eh, Ralston?"

While the others laughed, the man took out a pipe and planted it in between his teeth. Biting down on it, he pulled out a smooth-sided, old-fashioned lighter and brought it to flame. Pulling down with a deep breath, he let out a cloud of smoke and then said through its haze, "Novel, very novel. I'm sure no academic has ever thought of it before."

The others laughed again, young Carstairs telling them all that the day Professor Ralston needed to plagiarize from him was the day he would be feeling honored indeed.

As he did, Sam finished his mental checklist, thinking, And if there was something happening out in the Ether that I'm supposed to be fixing—something I can't see but that's headed toward me anyway—then Al should be here telling me about it. But he's not. And that is *very* wrong thing number three.

While the others headed into the hall, Sam held back, pointing toward Frellinberg's pipe and pleading a need for one last breath of fresh air. Everyone laughed again good-naturedly, even Frellinberg who shook his fist with mock theatrics, calling Ralston an "environmental wacko," threatening to prove his love of nature was really part of a deeply rooted Oedipal complex that had just begun to surface.

After that Frellinberg capped his pipe and joined the others heading inside. Only Klein remained behind with Sam. The two stared up into the nearly cloudless sky, both marveling at the beauty of the day. Klein spoke first, saying, "You seem a touch preoccupied today."

"Oh? And am I under the lens here, Herr Dok'tor?" asked Sam jokingly.

"No, of course not. But we are friends. I know there's no one in the state with a busier schedule than you. I was just wondering if it was catching up to you?"

"Not yet," answered Sam honestly. "But I'll let you know if it does."

"If you say so," answered Klein, giving Sam a sharp look. "I'll believe it. But I was listening to you back there. That was not the style I'm used to hearing when you dish it out."

Holding up one hand to keep Sam from interrupting, the man nodded his head twice, then said, "I'm not prying. If you're just a little more, shall we say, self-absorbed today than usual . . . that's fine. I'm not so much curious as to *what* it is that is filling your mind, as I am over its nature. Speculation? Speculate all you want. I was only making sure it was not more in the nature of *worry*."

You've got some sharp friends, Ralston, thought Sam. I'll certainly give you that much.

"Sounds like you actually do have me under a lens."

"No, no, but when I hear you actually debating a pup like Carstairs rather than simply putting him out of his misery, I start looking for reasons. I could see the corners of your eyes glazing. I could hear the little—what, eighth, tenth of a second—pauses before you responded. I know you, Mark. You were barely paying attention."

Very sharp.

"Anyway," started Klein again, angling his body toward the lecture hall as he placed one hand on Sam's arm, "every man has secrets, and he deserves to have them respected. As I said, I'm not prying, I'm just making sure that you're all right."

Sam reviewed his host's life again, looking for the least little thing that might be out of place. On the one hand, he knew he would not be living inside the professor's head if everything was fine. On the other, however, he could not point to anything that was out of place.

On that morning, looking up into the bright clear Nevada sky, Dr. Sam Beckett was more positive about Leaping than he had been in a long time. Despite his intensely painful Leap, despite the time out from his own life which Leaping meant, he had not been as happy with his accidental fate since . . .

Since never. I've never felt this good about Leaping, he thought honestly. On a day like this, I almost wish I could keep Leaping forever.

Then, as a surprisingly cool breeze felt its way across the campus, he amended the thought.

Strike the "almost." I do wish this would go on forever.

Looking up into the deep blue of the sky again, he added, I really do.

Then he opened his eyes, not wanting to put off his companion. Tilting his head to be able to look down into the shorter man's eyes, he said, "I appreciate the concern, Frank. I really do. But honestly, there is absolutely nothing wrong in my life right now." As the pair started into the lecture hall, he added, "In fact, I'd go so far as to say that there is no luckier man on the face of the earth right now than Professor Mark Ralston."

CHAPTER
ELEVEN

Al was headed back to the Imaging Chamber. The word he had been sent was that Ziggy was nearly back on-line. Which meant that the Project was almost ready to function once more. Which, most importantly to Al, meant that he could finally find out where Sam was.

Where he is, how he is, when he is, thought the admiral. His pace quickened. All of it.

Calm down, he told himself. You're going to end up giving yourself a heart attack.

Al felt an annoying tugging in his lungs. Slowing a fraction, he conceded that he knew he needed more rest, and that he also knew he needed to take it easy—at least for a while—and that there was only so much he could do and that he was aware that he had to let people do their jobs.

Yeah, yeah, yeah, he admitted to the badgering voice in his mind, I know all of the above. I also know that

I'm in charge. And that if I'm in charge, then that's as far as the buck goes. I can't push people any harder than I'm willing to push myself. And since I like pushing people to the max, I've really got no choice, have I?

Al's nagging voice, the one he usually referred to as Mama Gerstein, remained silent. He had given it that name because it was the part of his brain that, while it did bitch and moan and bellyache over every little thing he did, it did so with a distinct eye out for his well-being. It was the vocalization of his self-interest—the part of Al Calavicci dedicated to keeping him alive. His third mother-in-law had been like that; she always had a complaint ready for Al whenever she saw him, but he had always felt she had his best interests at heart.

Hell, if Ruthie had worried about me as much as her mother did, there probably wouldn't have been a fourth Mrs. Calavicci, let alone a fifth, Al thought.

As Al turned down the hall leading to the elevator to the lowest levels of the Project, he admitted that he was exaggerating. Ruthie had cared about him, but as time went by he had found ways to break things up. All in all, he was probably not really the marrying type.

"Hey," he said in a whisper, certain there was no one about to hear him talking to himself, but self-conscious nonetheless. "Sure I am. Five wives? I am most definitely the marrying type."

Stepping into a featureless, empty eight- by ten-foot room at the end of the hall, he closed the door behind him, saying in a louder voice, "I am definitely the marrying type." Then he added, "I'm just not the stay-married type."

Then, putting the whole subject aside, he said, "Down," bracing himself as the room dropped. He had grown used to the sensation so long ago he barely even noticed it anymore. Before Sam's first Leap he had timed the descent by counting in his head, the room always coming to a stop exactly at two hundred.

Now he spent the minute plus concentrating on the latest crisis, which was usually the same—worrying about how to get Sam back into his own body.

But this time the standard crisis has a few wrinkles, thought Al, drumming his fingers on the wall, waiting for the room to reach two hundred. As he felt the feather-soft landing, his hand reached for the door.

"Okay, so let's go out there and see if Gushie or Tina has learned how to iron."

Al's pace quickened with every step between the elevator and the Control Room. By the time he threw open the door, the back of his mind was again telling him to calm down. The admiral smiled. Mama Gerstein really did love him, didn't she?

"Al," said Tina. "I think we might have some good news for you."

Al wanted to show pleasure at her announcement, wanted to give everyone the impression that he had at least tried to be nice . . . in case things were not actually working yet, and he had to snap at people again—more harshly than normal . . . like the other day.

The other day? he thought. Who did I snap at the other day?

Al worried for a brief second. He had been having troublesome thoughts lately—thoughts that time might be shifting around him without him knowing it. He knew it was possible, and all morning he had been getting the hazy impression that he could *almost* remember such shifts taking place while he was within the Project.

Maybe, he told himself, because they've got Ziggy fixed, and part of me is there in Ziggy, maybe I'm sensing some of what the Zig picked up . . . remember more just because I'm connected to the big tin can.

Yeah, and maybe not. Who cares? If time is changing in faster and faster waves, then you should stop crying in your beer and get on with what you're supposed to be doing.

What other man, thought Al, his smile turning into a more twisted grin, ever agreed with their mother-in-law as often as I do?

"What's that smirk for?" asked Tina, seeing the change come over the admiral.

"You wouldn't believe me if I told you," he answered, "and I don't have time to tell you anyway. Sam's usually itchy if we take three or four minutes getting to him, and it's been four days. So, let's get this show on the road. Is Ziggy back with us or not?"

"Ask her yourself," said Gushie, pulling himself out of a floor compartment.

Thick bunches of bound cables were running up from the same dislocated section and a half dozen others. Some ran up into the ceiling, others off into the walls. Some were cut and patched into each other. Al swore he saw one that just was looped back into itself. Ignoring it, turning his attention completely away from the spiderweb the usually pristine Control Room had become, he said, "What's the word, Zig? Ready to get back to work?"

"I am feeling a bit more stable than I was ninety-three hours ago when the temporal surge first disabled me."

Al, who had just picked up his handlink, turned back toward the point of the room that he considered to be the computer's face. Looking from it to Tina, then to Gushie, then back to Ziggy, he asked, "What? A *temporal* surge? Time is like electricity all of a sudden? We're getting feedback trouble now?"

"It's hard to explain, Admiral," said Gushie. "We've been trying to figure it out . . . all three of us." He waved his hand about to indicate that he was including the computer along with himself and Tina. "And we haven't been having a whole lot of luck."

"This is one of those problems more along Dr. Beckett's lines," admitted Tina. She wiped at her brow, pushing the creeping line of perspiration back into her red hair. Despite the heating system, the lowest levels of the Project never seemed to lose their chill. And because of the nature of her equipment, Ziggy was kept cooler than anything else.

For Tina to be working up a sweat, thought Al, she must have really been busting her hump. But before he could allow her any particular credit for having done so, he reminded himself that they all were.

Let's not start thanking people just for doing their job, especially before we know whether or not they've done it right . . . no matter how much we want to take them to bed.

The admiral swept aside all of his complaints and worries. His first priority was getting to Sam. That was all that was important. With that in mind, he switched his handlink on, saying, "Feel that, Zig?" When the computer confirmed that the link felt as solid as always, Al said, "Okay, then that's just about all we need to know. Let me get a few things straight and I'll be on my way. Ziggy—I don't give a rat's ass as to what a temporal surge is . . . right now I don't even care how it happened. All I want to know is, is it fixed?"

"The damage seems to have been repaired quite adequately," Ziggy purred, a note of praise in her voice, not something the usually aloof computer was known for.

Wondering about that slightly, Al asked, "Do you think it can happen again? Do you think it can do anything to throw off me getting back to Sam? And do you think it did anything to Sam?"

"I have to impress upon you, Admiral, that we are not really sure as to the nature of the surge. We know it was not merely a thing of this physical reality. It was something out of the time stream. Perhaps a glitch or feedback of some sort—given the currentlike nature of the temporal field Dr. Beckett has tapped into, your electrical analogy is not unwarranted—was responsible. My theory, however, tends away from random chance and more toward a guiding hand."

"Meaning . . . ?" asked Al warily.

"Meaning that I feel quite strongly that Dr. Beckett was hit by something previously unexperienced by us. I feel that it most likely was as painful and disorienting for him as it was for me. I do not feel, though, that it will prevent you from reaching him.''

"Why not?'' asked Al, his eyes running over the colored lights of his handlink to Ziggy, checking their levels.

"Because if whatever did this to us did not want you to reach Dr. Beckett, it would not have allowed me to be repaired.''

Al squinted one eye until only a thin field of vision remained. He stared at the computer, wondering where she had come up with her latest ideas.

"Ziggy,'' he asked, "have you suddenly gone out and gotten religion on us?''

"Do I believe in forces beyond myself, beyond even Dr. Beckett, my creator?'' The computer answered with questions, then answered them before anyone else could. "Yes, Admiral . . . I do. Obviously Dr. Beckett stepped into the Accelerator and experienced something none of us, not even he, can explain. So, yes, Admiral, I do believe in forces beyond any we can explain.'' Then the computer's voice took on her usual condescending tone.

"I do not presume to understand them, of course. Nor do I claim any special ability toward being able to furnish detailed descriptions of them. That I leave to your prelates.''

"Okay, you haven't gotten religion but you do believe in the Twilight Zone,'' said Al, relieved by hearing Ziggy sound more like herself. "Fine enough. Whatever makes a person happy, I always say. Even you, Zig.''

"Thank you, Admiral. Will you be going now? I believe I am ready to provide my usual services.''

"Have you located Sam?"

"Yes. He has come forward since his last Leap to 1986."

Al grinned, relief flooding his body. Turning back to Tina and Gushie, he said, "Looks like you two have done a good job. Thanks. But now, if you'll excuse me, I have a door to catch."

"Which door would you like, Admiral?"

Al turned back toward the computer—sharply. Anxiety flooded him anew, more powerful and troubling than before. Ziggy had switched back to the accommodating, helpful voice—the one the admiral decided he did not trust one bit.

"What do you mean, which door? What are you talking about? I thought you said you'd located Sam?"

"I have, Admiral. He is in Reno, Nevada. The date is the fourteenth of May, 1986."

Al stood staring at the computer, not bothering to ask it any questions. As Tina and Gushie moved up behind him, also staring, also not saying anything, Ziggy finally let the other shoe drop, saying, "And he is also outside of Elko, Nevada, heading toward Carlin. The date is the fourteenth of May, 1986."

Al stood for a long moment, not knowing what to say. Finally, though, he ordered, "Pick one and send me back."

Without comment, Ziggy settled down to work, as Al entered the Imaging Chamber. The computer allowed a random sequence to pick one of the two possible destinations she had for Dr. Beckett. Then she began running through the series of commands which would place Al at his side.

When nothing happened, the computer tried sending the admiral to the other point instead. When nothing happened again, Ziggy admitted, "I am afraid I must announce that I do not appear to be able to provide my usual services after all."

For four days Al Calavicci had thought he had understood just how anxious, just how worried he could grow over Sam's fate. At that moment, however, he realized he had not even begun to know what true fear was all about.

CHAPTER
TWELVE

Sam pushed down on the gas pedal, feeding fuel to the massive rig. There was an incline coming and he did not feel like losing a fraction of speed.

Why should I? he asked himself rhetorically. Why should I slow down for anything or wait for anyone? Ever again?

His mouth drew into a thin line as he fed the truck more gas, shifting upward through the gears. Now that he had claimed Ward Ralston's life for his own, he was impatient to get on with it. Only a fool spent time on the road when he had a loving family to get home to.

"And Sam Beckett," he said, correcting himself after taking a long swig from his thermos of hot black coffee, "I *mean*, Ward Ralston . . . is nobody's fool. Not anymore, anyway. And if I have any say so—and I do—not ever again."

Sam noted that Ward's accent had begun to disappear.

Throughout his Leaps, he usually spoke like whoever he was at the moment. Just as they "saw" his host, they "heard" his host as well. Sam had not been surprised to hear the hard G -dropping tones of Ward's voice when he first spoke to Betty.

But now that he had decided to forget about looking for something to fix in Ward's life, he found the man's accent slipping away. In fact, the last time he had spoken to anyone, it had been gone entirely.

And what a conversation *that* had been, Sam chuckled to himself.

It had been in Tahoe, at his last stop before heading back to Portland. He had found the delivery site marked on his manifest easily enough. The store owner had gotten his workers on the job quickly, and they had almost finished getting the last of the load off before Sam discovered that there were pockets of Ward Ralston's life he hadn't turned inside-out yet.

"Now what, pray tell, were you going to do?" she asked. Her voice poured over him in a warm purr, one deepened to just the right tone by the perfect number of raw whiskey shots over the years.

"Excuse me?" Sam asked. When he turned he had found a woman of twenty-one, -two—no, maybe twenty-six, -seven even. Her skin and hair had a girl's luster but her eyes held a depth that was much older, and much wiser.

While Sam took her in with his eyes, liking what he saw—liking it a great deal—she stared back. It was a look he had grown to recognize during his Leaps. It told him that not only did he know the young beauty sizing him up, but that he knew her quite well. Before he could say anything further, the woman smiled.

"Ward Ralston, I don't believe you have looked at me like that in quite some time."

"Like what?" he asked, still trying to figure out *how* quite well they knew each other.

The woman moved closer to him, backing him away from his truck toward the building beyond. Her eyes widened just a trace to see him take the involuntary step. Beaming, she answered, "Like *what*? Like *that*. Like all of a sudden you weren't so full of yourself—as usual. Like you were happy to see me."

"Well," answered Sam honestly, his eyes running up from her long legs over her well-filled-out form, noting her long dark hair, locking on her deep brown eyes, "I can't imagine any man who wouldn't be happy to see you. Maybe a few from San Francisco, but other than that . . ."

"Oh, Ward," she giggled, "you are such a naughty naughty man."

The next thing she did was to move forward on Sam, herding him toward a more private spot. Trying to get some kind of a handle on things, he told her—hoping he was reminding her—that he was a married man. She took the comment as a joke. Not that he was joking about actually being married, but that he was joking over thinking she cared. He bantered with her for a few more minutes, quickly realizing that she—one Miss Ellen Moore—had been waiting for Ward to arrive all day. She was his Tahoe girl. Whenever he was in town, he was hers.

Sam was astounded at her sensibilities. Not only did Ward's marriage mean nothing to her, but neither did the women he apparently had in every other town along his favorite circuits. It seemed the last time he had been in Tahoe, Ward had spent much of their night drinking and comparing Ellen to the others on his route—quite unfavorably to many of them.

She had decided to get herself decked out for him this time, to see if his opinion had changed any. Embarrassed, Sam hid behind the kind of rough exterior he knew he could get away with as Ward, fumbling for an avenue of escape. Part of him worked at maintaining his new identity—

Wouldn't do for people to start questioning what was wrong with Ward. Making him nicer is one thing; making him *too* nice could expose the whole show.

—while part of him tried to ease his way out of the situation entirely. He did not want to lose a customer as valuable as her employer. He also did not want an angry call going to Portland to blow up the life he was trying to steal.

"I'm not stealing it," he said angrily, pushing his rig up over the top of the rise. "Ward Ralston is a shit. He doesn't deserve this life."

"And you do?" asked a dubious voice in Sam's head.

"Yes," he snarled, spitting the word out. "Yes I do."

Ellen was clearly disappointed, but Leaping had taught Sam a great deal about lying without getting caught or hurting people's feelings. He had managed to do both.

He rambled on about thinking she would never want

to see him again, that he had not brought the present he usually did because he had come to realize he was only using her—and that it was wrong to use people. And then, sensing that she knew she was being snowed—covered in the kind of treacle reserved for chumps and fools, Sam shifted gears, letting her know that "the truth" was he just had to get back on the road. His next run was a big money job and taking it on had left him absolutely no time at all. He had to get back to Portland, take care of business, and get to it.

"Much as I hate leaving the sight of you behind, my sweet dish of sugar candy," he drawled, amused and annoyed with the situation at the same time, "I gotta get moving. Got to pedal the metal and suck some bucks." Shifting his voice down suggestively, he added, "But I will be back."

"Oh, I know you will," she said, her voice filled with tease. Before Sam could turn away, her hands slid up the edges of her collar and pulled open her blouse. Sam stared a great deal longer than he thought Ward Ralston might have—so long he felt blood rising in his cheeks.

She turned and disappeared back into the building behind them, her blouse rebuttoned before Sam could even raise his hand to give her a wave good-bye. After that, he returned to his truck, got his manifest back from the loading dock boss stamped ACCEPTED, and pulled himself up into his cab, glad to be on his way out of Lake Tahoe.

Hours later, however, he was wondering if he should have made such a hasty retreat. After all, he was giving up a lot to step down into being Ward Ralston. Shouldn't

97

he be entitled to whatever rewards came with this new life?

Shocked, Sam glanced at himself in the rearview mirror, as though looking for reassurances. Don't worry about it so much, he thought. Those were Ward's thoughts, not yours. You may look like Ward Ralston, but you're not. And you're not going to have the crummy life he did.

It was true. Ward did things like play around with Ellen because he was not the man Sam Beckett was. Sam was not about to let a beautiful, caring woman like Betty Ralston suffer any longer. Nor was he going to neglect Taylor or Barbara. Leaping, Sam had missed out on family—on love. He was not about to miss out on any more of it.

But how can I have that if I'm always on the road, always away from them? That was half of Ward's problem. If he'd been home where he belonged, women like Ellen wouldn't be such a temptation. But how can I take care of my family if I quit this job?

Sam was lost in thought as the automatic portion of his brain worked the gears and pedals, watching his speed, on the alert for the state police.

It's '86. Elections coming up. Super Bowl. Academy Awards. Every fact I ever saw in any newspaper. It's all in my head. All I have to do is find some suckers and get those bets placed. Make some *real* money. Mortgage the house—sell the rig. What's the difference? It's not like the Ralstons' being wealthy is going to affect the time/space continuum any more than I already have.

The changes he'd make in Ward's life weren't going

98

to change who became the president of the United States, governor of New Mexico. Who won best actor or the World Series. And if it did . . . well, the world evolved. Change is the only constant, wasn't that the phrase?

As far as he knew, Sam had never thought like this before. Of course, he had never tried to hijack a Leap before, either. As the hours wore on, as he passed from Nevada into northern California and then into Oregon, as afternoon became evening, pushing on toward the next day, Sam found himself unable to stop thinking about what he could do to change Ward's life into one more to his liking.

Place bets? Certainly. Why not? But also, why not buy a keyboard and join a band? He knew where music was heading over the next eight years. And he knew he had musical talent. Cash-in city. Or go into computer network servicing—he had a nice jump on that market, too. Eight years of future history wasn't much to most men, but he was Sam Beckett. His only problem would be explaining how a nobody like Ward Ralston became so, so . . .

"So much like Sam Beckett?" He could not help laughing out loud after he said the words, but the laughter was a bit edgy. He was getting road-weary. Where Sam Beckett might have pushed on, hoping to cut some time off his trip, Ward Ralston's instincts knew better.

Ralston had mapped out his route with a layover in Grant's Pass. His reservation was already made. Checking the map, Sam figured home to be at least two hundred more miles away—two hundred miles of moving a multiple-ton, eighteen-wheeled vehicle over mountain roads at night.

"All right," he said, seeing the exit sign for Grant's Pass. "No sense in killing ourselves."

He pulled into the parking lot of the Stop On Inn fifteen minutes later. Locking his truck up in the section set aside for the long-distance trade that frequented Route 5, Sam made his way to the front office. His body ached from manhandling the rig up out of the desert and into the mountains.

Maybe Ward might have been able to make it all the way back to Portland with no trouble, if he'd wanted, thought Sam, but I'm dead tired. Besides, I've already conceded that he's the pro here. If he thinks stopping is a good idea . . . He stretched his arms over his head, pain shooting through each vertebra in his spine.

"Then so do I."

Kicking some of the dust from his boots, Sam stepped up onto the porch of the motel's office and made his way inside. At first it appeared no one was on duty, but a curl of cigarette smoke coming up from behind the manager's wall assured him someone was present. Moving across the rug to the front desk, he said, "Hi. I believe I have a reservation."

A woman stood up into sight in response to his voice.

"You sure took your good, sweet time getting here."

Sam looked at the woman. She was older than Ellen Moore, a bit heavier in spots here and there, but more attractive overall. She wore a layer of makeup designed to give her that no-makeup look, one that went well with her high cheekbones and full lips. She had long, full wavy brown hair, big brandy brown eyes, and a look that told Sam a lot about Ward Ralston.

The woman reached for Sam over the counter, catching hold of him and dragging him up against its steel edge. As their lips made contact, Sam thought, Oh, boy . . .

CHAPTER

THIRTEEN

It had been a long day. Mark Ralston did not teach boring classes. Nor were any of his students looking for a set of fluff credits. He tackled tough subjects in a frank manner, making no excuses nor dismissing any degree of responsibility.

That's for sure, thought Sam, nodding his head absently. At least, not if the way his students hung on every word I said all day is any evidence of the way he's trained them to respond.

Sam had not found a slacker in any of Ralston's classes. Some students were better than others—such was only natural and he had expected it. But after what he had heard and read over the years about the state of the country's university enrollees, he had also expected at least a small percentage of his students to be "get-bys"—those with far less mastery of the skills needed when he was college age to get into even the most basic state-run university.

But that had not been the case, not even in his Introduction to the Workings of the Human Mind, the title of a *cake* course if he had ever heard one. The auditorium assembly he had been addressing every other morning at 8:30 was as eager to learn as any he had ever seen.

He had lectured on the separate properties and responsibilities of the left and right brain that morning. On a lark, he had emphasized the additions to that debate that had been made by some of the scholars regarded as more from the fringe of Ralston's chosen science rather than from its vanguard. Men like the British philosopher and science fiction writer Colin Wilson.

Sam had been gratified to see that the name was recognized by more than half the class. In an introductory, undergraduate course like Human Mind, to find so many of his students that well versed with someone from outside the field of study gave him the feeling that the next generation coming up might not be as unprepared as the media kept insisting.

He wanted to throw out Ralston's prepared course outline and run wild—to see just how much the students might actually know, but he restrained himself. Even though his current Leap was not progressing in what passed for a normal manner, that was no excuse to disrupt the professor's life. There was no telling exactly when Mark Ralston was going to return and Sam was going to move on.

To experiment with another man's existence just for

the fun of it . . . Sam let the thought trail off in his mind, horrified. He was amazed that he could even consider such a thing.

But hadn't there been times already when he had experimented with the past? Yes. Some he remembered, and he had no idea how many he'd forgotten. That was why he was here. He had Leaped into Mark Ralston's existence to change something. But without Al and Ziggy to guide him, he didn't know what that change was supposed to be. Just because he had the urge to play professor didn't mean that what he was here to change was the direction of Ralston's classes. Well, it could be, but without any proof, he decided to simply stick to interpreting Abraham Maslow's *Motivation and Personality* for the time being.

He got the class in and out of the material with ease— assigning everyone Maslow's "five point hierarchy of needs" for discussion when next they gathered just as the period ended.

After that, he headed for Ralston's office and met with each of the thirty-five students who showed up looking for him. He listened to them intently, looking for anything that might give him a clue as to why he had been inserted into the professor's life. But none of them appeared to be in any of the kinds of trouble he was normally sent to correct.

It figures, Sam thought with a great deal of disgust. Either I Leap into something in progress, or I spend my time blundering around looking for clues. Why isn't there ever any middle ground? And, Al, where are you?

•   •   •

After his hours were over, Professor Klein stopped by to pick him up for their meeting. Both of them were in the same environmental group. Sam had been granted two breaks on that one. Despite Ralston's normally scrupulous record keeping, appointment noting, meeting schedules, et cetera, he had not noted the environmental gathering. Klein had made mention of it during their walk earlier in the day, which had been Sam's first break. The second was that it was Klein's turn to drive.

The shorter man had picked Sam up at his office, rescuing him from three undergraduates determined to argue him into the ground over Maslow's relevance to current times.

As he and Klein pulled out of the faculty parking lot, he told the older man once more, "Thanks again for the rescue, Frank."

"Think nothing of it," answered the shorter man absently, growing impatient as he waited for a chance to move his Toyota station wagon out into the heavy evening traffic. "To tell you the honest truth, I was surprised you let me tear you away from your three stooges and their 'Maslow didn't go far enough' debate."

Spotting a hole in the blocking traffic stream, Klein made his move out into the lane.

"I don't mean to go on about it, but I have to say it's not really like you to cut off a student just because you have other duties."

"Well," said Sam, hoping his explanation would sound like something Mark Ralston would say, "when everything you're doing is of equal importance"—he shrugged—"about the only thing that can decide the matter is what time it is. You know—if you gotta go, then . . ." He paused for just a second, giving Klein time to come in with him. The doctor took his cue, joining Sam as he said, "You gotta go."

After the two finished chuckling, Klein signaled a left turn and then eased his station wagon into it with much less energy than he had used to make his mad dash out of the parking lot, saying, "My God, Mark—there may be hope for you yet."

"You make me sound like I should be paying you by the hour."

"Not a bad idea," answered Klein with mock seriousness. "I could have Nancy schedule you for Thursdays."

"Ha . . . ha. You're a riot, Herr Dok'tor."

"Why," answered Klein with a sly tone, "you make it sound as if we hit a nerve." The doctor laughed again, then said, "Whatever. Listen, Mark, all I meant was it was good to see you ease up for just a moment. You may not have noticed, but you do tend to drive yourself a bit."

Yes, thought Sam, Mark Ralston tends to drive himself two or three bits. Easy.

And maybe that's Ralston's problem. Maybe we're here to get him to relax a little. Or break that caffeine habit of his. It's not the kind of luck we usually have, but it would be a nice change.

Yes, it certainly would be.

"Daydreaming? Not like you, Mark."

"Oh, you know, just thinking . . ."

"Do you mean," asked Klein, an unusually loud note

of interest in his voice, "about things like tonight's meeting?"

"What do you mean, Frank?" asked Sam, hoping he could get the doctor to tell him what was going to be going on before he got there and ended up on the spot.

"I mean that Penzler's promised to have his report ready," answered the driver with a touch of hesitation. "The report you've been waiting for for two months— that we've been waiting for for six years."

Darn, thought Sam, he's talking about the one part of Ralston's life that he did not keep scrupulously recorded. Everything else is notated to the last decimal—everything but *this*. And from the way Klein keeps eyeing me whenever he can turn away from the traffic, I have a feeling this should be a lot more important than price listings on the German pewter that's available on the market.

Hoping his lost-in-thought excuse could continue to cover him, Sam feebly offered, "I'm sorry, Frank. I, well . . . I haven't really been able to check my notes recently . . ."

"Notes?" asked Klein harshly, his fingers tightening around the steering wheel. "What in the name of God would you need notes for? Why would you even write anything down? We agreed to not keep any personal records . . ." The doctor wheezed and then coughed.

Catching his breath, he continued, "What's wrong with you, Mark? You do remember Oregon Removal & Transport, don't you? Cleaning up toxic sites, handling dumping for steel companies, chrome makers, chemical processors, nuclear facilities—most of them known polluters . . . does any of this ring a bell?''

Sam held his hands to the sides of his head, attempting to use mock confusion to hide his actual ignorance. Letting his eyes glaze over, he answered sarcastically, hoping to goad Klein into dropping the other shoe, ''Ah, maybe a tiny bell.''

''I have two words for you, Professor,'' answered Klein, regaining his good humor, ''one is a verb, the other a pronoun. A tiny bell. We finally have a chance to nail these bastards, and you make jokes.''

''Well,'' said Sam, praying for Klein to keep talking. ''You know.''

''Yes, I know. I know that if they get away with making this next dump we've gotten word of that . . . that . . . Good Lord in heaven, man . . . I mean . . .'' He turned to face Sam for a split second as he asked, ''What does one say . . . can one say about a crime of this magnitude?''

Suddenly Sam realized that perhaps there was indeed something going on in Mark Ralston's life that might need some kind of outside attention.

''If what Penzler thinks is true, thousands could be affected. Hundreds of thousands. Who knows how many? Perhaps millions. Millions. Condemned to unstoppable pain and irreversible death. I mean, what words do you use to even begin to describe such a thing?''

This was it. Sam was certain, as Klein answered his own question.

''Holocaust. That's the word you use. Holocaust.''

CHAPTER
FOURTEEN

Al sat in the cafeteria, drumming his fingers. He had kept his temper in both the Imaging Chamber and the Control Room. He had told himself that it was not Ziggy's fault she could not send Al back to Sam. Nor was it either Tina's or Gushie's. The chief engineer and head programmer had gone over everything—twice. They had Ziggy back on-line . . . she could do anything she could before her "blackout."

Anything except send the admiral through the door. Anything but get him to Sam.

But why not? wondered Al, the voice in his head harsh and cold. Because suddenly . . . not only can she locate Sam, she's locating him everywhere.

"Ziggy, Ziggy, how could you do this to us?" the admiral muttered under his breath. "First you can't find Sam at all, so to make up for it you find me two of him. How many millions did you cost the taxpayers? Whatever it was, it was too much.''

Al watched his fingers. He knew that there were far more important things he could be doing. Maybe even that he *should* be doing. But he also knew there was nothing more important than getting back to Sam and his inability to do that was pushing him slowly toward the edge. He had begun to calm down when he first heard that Ziggy was running again. But when the computer had failed to pinpoint Sam, failed to get the two of them together again, his tenuous control had snapped.

The admiral had not screamed at anyone, nor had he thrown anything. Not only did he not raise his voice, he barely spoke. All he had done was tersely turn to Gushie and growl quietly, ''Work on it.''

And then he had left, heading straight for the cafeteria. At first he had thought of returning to his quarters to get his hot mug. A sudden urge had filled him to take the dozen cups of coffee it could hold and go up to the surface and just sit. It was a crazy idea, to go up into the baking heat of the broiling New Mexico sun and drink hot coffee. But it made as much sense as some of the other things that had been happening, and he had been sorely tempted.

In the end, however, he had not done it. Not gone outside, not gone to his quarters for his hot mug, not had a cup of coffee. Not even hidden himself in his closet of an office and had a rare, solitary drink. In fact, even though he did go to the cafeteria, he did not eat or drink anything at all.

The small yellow plastic tray he had taken still sat in front of him, still held the microwaved pizza burger and the slice of chocolate cake, and the glass of water. All of it untouched—even the water—his hands stretched out on either side of the tray, too busy drumming to bother with anything else.

Al watched as his fingers rose and fell. He noted that his pinkie fingers hit first, followed down the row by each of the others until all four on each hand had struck the tabletop. Then it would begin again. He counted off how many times he could do it within a minute, timing himself by keeping one eye on the wall clock and one on his hands. Out of eighteen tries his best score was two hundred eighty-seven.

As he continued to watch his fingers, he noted that his thumbs never touched the table. They remained roughly a half an inch above, only wavering slightly whenever his drumming intensified, but never actually touching. He also noted that he always started with the pinkie.

I wonder if it can be done in reverse?

He tried it with just one hand first, forcing the index finger of his left hand down, the other three following stiffly. The experiment did not work well. Although he was able to bang out an awkward rhythm: index, middle, ring, pinkie . . . index, middle, ring, pinkie, he could neither do it smoothly nor with any great speed.

Then, just as quickly as he had started his finger-drumming marathon, he stopped. He lay his hands palm down on the table, one to either side of his tray, and simply stared at them. He didn't bother to keep track of how long he sat there. It didn't matter. Nothing mattered, except getting to his best friend—and that was the one thing in the world he could not do.

Tired of going in circles with the same complaints, Al grabbed up the long-cooled pizza burger, biting at it—chewing without tasting. Swallowing without noticing.

Al's mind was whirling, searching desperately for any kind of answer to the Project's latest disaster. It was his duty to figure things like this out. His and his alone. He was in charge and the responsibility for containing disasters was always the top dog's.

No way to delegate this one. No way out of the cage.

Al looked down absently, noticing that he was licking his fingers. A quick scan showed him his tray was empty, even his water glass was empty. He sighed, wondering how many times he ate meals anymore without even noticing.

"Hell," he said aloud, "I wonder when I started thinking of this crap as actual meals?"

Standing up, he moved around his chair, pushed it back in, and then headed over to the waste bin to throw away his trash. Leaving his tray atop the bin, he moved out into the hall. He walked slowly. Eventually, for lack of any better ideas, he started moving toward the Waiting Room.

Maybe Beeks has finally gotten through to whoever it is lying there inside Sam's skull, he thought. Maybe whoever it is can help us get a hold on why we can't get through to Sam.

Al entered the Waiting Room with little enthusiasm. He was pleased to a small extent to see Dr. Beeks bending over Sam, but was not heartened by the sight when she moved enough for him to see the body. Sam was still not moving. Not a toe or a finger.

"I take it whoever's playing house in Sam these days isn't just asleep."

"You take it right, Admiral." The doctor turned around to stare at Al. He swore that if anything, she looked even more worn out than he did. Dropping into a chair next to the bed holding Sam's body, she said wearily, "Yo sure 'nough takin' it right there, honey chile."

"Oh, great," answered Al with a sour look. "Just great. We're all slipping our noodle here. Okay, I can deal with it."

Slipping into an accent that sounded more *Godfather* than anything else, he said, "Tell you what, Verbeena, doll . . . you 'n me, we should work up an act for the talent show."

With that, Al clasped his hands over his heart and let loose with a few lines of "Volare." As Beeks laughed, he opened his eyes, unclasped his hands, and shrugged. "No, huh?"

"No offense, Admiral," answered the black woman with a smile, grateful for even the smallest thing to distract her from the problem before her, "but I don't think either one of us had better give up their day job."

"I don't know," answered Al, staring past her at Sam's unmoving form. "If things keep going like they are, we might be out looking for new day jobs."

The admiral circled the bed, feeling even more restless than when he had been drumming his fingers in the cafeteria. Sliding his hand along the tube of an IV bottle hanging next to the bed, the end of which disappeared into Sam's arm, Al asked, "Nutrition?"

"He can't eat on his own . . ." Beeks let the words trail off. She knew the admiral understood. He was simply tired of the quiet. Shaking off her own exhaustion, she tried to fill it in for him, saying, "I heard about Ziggy not being able to center you on Sam. And, what else? It was something strange. Oh, yes . . . it was something about Ziggy having two locations for Dr. Beckett instead of one."

"Right on both counts," Al admitted, flopping into a chair of his own. "So, with nothing going on anywhere else, I thought I'd come in here and see how you were doing."

"Oh, everything in here is just fine," Beeks answered with a sigh. Waving her hand over Sam's unmoving body, she said, "As you can see."

"I assume he's . . . Sam, I mean . . . that he's okay, and all. Still. Right?"

"Don't get flustered, Admiral," said the doctor in a calming tone. "I've kept close tabs on him. So far all his readings are well within what I've come to think of as normal parameters. It's typical, when someone new comes in, for certain levels to change a bit, but it's never anything to get alarmed about. And it's the same now. Heart rate, blood pressure, motor responses, saliva output, brain waves—all within the normal parameters. Other than his not responding to us, everything's fine."

Al sat, staring at Sam. He heard everything the doctor told him, but he did not answer. Sitting with his chin in the palm of his left hand, he just kept staring, waiting for some sort of idea to hit him—or a miracle. Whichever one cared to strike first.

"I suppose," he said absently, thinking out loud, "you've tried everything in the way of stimulants that you can—right?"

Now it was Dr. Beek's turn to not answer. Al noticed the silence. He raised his voice and asked again, "Right?"

"Yes, yes," she snapped, slightly annoyed at being prodded. "There's just not very much that we can risk. Especially not one after another. If something doesn't work I have to give it time to dissipate. Over the past few days, of course, I've had plenty of time. I've given him a series of antidepressants, stimulants . . . I even tried a shot of adrenaline, but that was as far as I dared go."

"And no response—even with adrenaline?"

"Not much. A little more intense REM activity, but nothing to write home about." Before Al could respond, the doctor crossed her arms over her chest, announcing, "And that's as far as I'm going. Understand?"

"Wha—what do you mean?"

"I mean that I'm not going to give him anything stronger, that I'm not going to double the dose, or try anything experimental. That I'm not going to put my patient at any further risk." Standing like a soldier expecting a dressing down, she stared at the motionless body, her hands raising as though to touch him. She pulled back, forcing her arms to relax at her side, and let out a painful breath.

"I'm sorry, Al. I didn't mean to snap at you. It's just that I know so damn little about what's safe and what isn't. You understand, don't you? It's not like I can pull an issue of the *American Medical Journal* off the shelf and thumb to the section on reviving the guest chamber section of the brain for the temporary residents within time travelers.''

Verbeena Beeks dropped her arms to her sides, shoulders sagging as she turned to face the admiral, one elegant hand gesturing helplessly.

''This isn't easy, you know?''

Al nodded, slouching farther into his chair.

''It's all right,'' he reassured her. ''Trust me, nobody here knows how you feel any better than me.''

''If there was only something we could do for him. Something else left to try. If we just even had another idea.'' She looked so despondent that Al forgot his role as Project ass-kicker, standing to draw her into his arms, giving what comfort he could. She shut her eyes for a moment, forgetting where she was, whose arms she was in. She held on to Al, taking what strength he had to offer.

Not feeling uncomfortable in the least, Al continued to hold her gently. He knew such moments all too well after five marriages, knew how long one should last with any woman to within ten seconds. Knowing Beeks was good for another moment, he looked over her shoulder at Sam again, still prone on the bed, still breathing quietly. To fill the silence, he said, ''Like I said before, in the old days, when someone in my chain of command looked like Sam there, all we needed was a pot of black coffee to get them back on their feet. I sure as hell know it worked for me." He smiled a little, remembering a young sailor named Bingo.

Verbeena Beeks went stiff in Al's arms. The admiral backed away a few inches. Still holding on to the woman's arms, he asked, "Verbeena . . . are you okay?"

"Why not?"

"What?"

"Coffee."

"What is it?" asked Al with sudden interest.

The admiral looked into Beeks's eyes, searching for an answer. She wasn't seeing him, her eyes glazing over as her well-trained mind ran over endless possibilities. Upset at being left out of the loop, Al shook the doctor gently, asking, "Verbeena—what is it? Do you want a cup of coffee? Talk to me, woman!"

Her eyes snapped back into focus. She stared at him for only a split second, then rapped against his chest with one hand. "Yes," she said emphatically. "Yes. Right away. Get down to the cafeteria and get me a big cup."

When Al did not move immediately, she snapped, "Now, damnit! Hurry."

Al felt as if he had been slapped. He released his hold on Beeks. He blinked in confusion. That tone was not Verbeena at all.

"Ah, always glad as I am to help out . . . can you maybe tell me what you want, I mean, with a cup of coffee?"

"It's not for me, you idiot," she answered, rolling her eyes as she turned away. Moving across the room, she started ripping open drawers, searching for something. Over her shoulder she yelled out, "It's for Sam."

117

Oh, of course, thought Al, stepping out into the hall. It's not for her—it's for Sam. Maybe Verbeena had gone off the deep end, but then, what the hell did they have to lose?

Admiral Al Calavicci started running, trying to get to the cafeteria as fast as possible.

CHAPTER
FIFTEEN

Sam slid his key into the front lock of Ward Ralston's home. He turned the knob and then pushed the door quietly, trying to enter without anyone noticing. He was shaking and nervous. His insides were tied in knots, stomach cramps brought on by a fierce attack of guilt.

Not that he had not enjoyed himself at the Stop On Inn—he had, more than he had ever thought possible. The delightful brunette had seen to that. Sam Beckett's problem was, however, that he had in the past always been able to stand pretty firmly on the rock-firm strata on which he grounded his moral standards. And now that foundation had begun to feel more like sand than granite during the drive back up to Portland.

He could rationalize his actions, had in fact been doing that, but nothing made it less reprehensible. For that one night, he had let Wade Ralston dictate his actions. Had *been* Wade Ralston, with no concern for anyone

119

other than himself and his own needs. Had been, in fact, a selfish, cheating bastard.

Sam reached up to straighten his cap. It was one he had found in the truck's glove compartment—a bright orange baseball cap marked "Jack's Gun Shop." It sported a picture of a broadly smiling skunk, which was just appropriate enough to make Sam put it on. It was how he had felt, arguing with himself while he drove home, trying to drown out the sound of his condemning thoughts.

Betty's not my wife, he said in self-defense. If Ward sleeps with someone else it's cheating. *I* didn't make any vows. Only he had, of course. He had vowed to do a better job with Ward's life than Ward had done. Well, you're off to a fine start then, aren't you? he sneered.

Finally, by the time he had made the turnoff for Portland, the small battles had begun to kindle a temper within him he had never felt before.

"Goddamnit," he roared, banging his fist down brutally against the dashboard. "Leave me alone! Just leave me the hell alone."

Why? So you can sneak in and let her see the fact that you've cheated written all over your face? Why not just pull over and get a bottle?

"Leave it . . ." Sam snarled.

That would be better, don't you think? After all, you want to steal Ward Ralston's life, then go ahead—steal it all. Get drunk and go home and slap everyone around a little.

"Stop . . ."

Go on . . . do it. Prove you're a real man for once,

120

Sam. Drinking, screwing, fun stuff. A little wife abuse, some screaming at the kids . . .

Sam's right foot slammed down on the brake, hard, and his knee locked painfully. He swore loudly, the truck shimmying to a halt around him. Car brakes squealed behind him, but he did not notice anything except the relentless voice berating him. Holding his throbbing head, he pleaded, "Just leave me alone."

Several of the motorists who had been forced to stop by his sudden braking had gotten out of their cars. One was nearing his cab, the others were looking on in interest. Catching notice of them in his side-view mirror, Sam suddenly realized what he had done—what he had almost done. Leaning out the window, he waved them all back, shouting, "I'm all right. Is everyone back there all right?"

"Yeah," answered the closest driver—a large man, brutish and angry. "And you're one lucky asshole for that. What the hell did you think you were doin', you moron?"

"Dog," lied Sam, not able to think of anything better. "Jumped out and then jumped back. Caught me off guard."

"A dog?" yelled the approaching man with shock. "You almost killed us over a damn dog?"

"I'm sorry," Sam shouted, pulling his head back into the cab. Grabbing at the gear shift, he yelled out before anyone could think to challenge him further, "I'll get out of the way right now. Sorry again. Sorry."

Then he had driven off, quickly before his troubles could deepen any further. As he made his way back to

Ward Ralston's home, however, he was grateful that the nagging voice had gone silent.

But in that silence came the questions. Why was he acting this way? What was it that was bothering him?

Great, thought Sam. Which possibility should I pick from the checklist? That I'm stealing a man's life? That I want his wife and kids because I'm never going to have any of my own? That I cheated on his wife?

It wasn't until Sam was outside of Ward Ralston's house that it hit him.

He was upset, not because he had slept with the brunette at the Stop On In.

He was upset because he'd *enjoyed* the cheating.

Not knowing what he would do—what he *could* do when he went inside—Sam tried to enter the house quietly. He knew he could not avoid the family, but he did not know what his reaction would be when he saw them . . . when he saw *her*, and he wanted to put it off as long as possible.

"Ward, honey?" came Betty's voice as he made his first step through the door. "Is that you?"

"No one else, sweetheart."

Sam listened to his voice. He sounded nervous. Before he could add anything, Betty came into the living room.

Sam whistled. If it were possible, she somehow seemed even more beautiful than the last time he had seen her. There was a change to her, something he could not put his finger on . . . something that made him want Ward Ralston's life even more than before.

This guy messed up for sure, thought Sam. What the

heck has changed about her, anyway?

He fretted for a moment over what had once been his perfect memory. Even with the Swiss-cheese effect between Leaps, he could usually remember things within a Leap. Now, however, he was staring at a woman he had just seen a few days earlier—*knowing* that there was something different about her—and yet not able to put his finger on what that difference might be.

Falling into the time-honored stalling ploy of husbands from all times, he said, "There's something different about you."

Betty only blushed, giving him the time-honored answer to his ploy. Left to guessing, he did his best, running through all the obvious choices first. It was not her hair—he was certain that was still styled the same. Her outfit did not look new, either, nor did her nails. The shoes she had on looked as old as everything else she was wearing.

Betty turned back and forth for him, spinning around once, her arms outstretched and a smile on her face. Seeing how perplexed he was, she took pity on him.

"Ward—oh, baby. Oh, you big, silly, wonderful man. It's not anything like my hair or blouse, or, or . . . or anything. It's *me*. It's all of me."

Then he understood. This was Betty's reaction to the new, improved Ward Ralston. He had been playing to her hopes and dreams and had dispelled all her worst fears. Suddenly she no longer had to dread growing old. She was not going to end her days a single mother with two children and no future. She was not going to be a woman who stayed bound to an abusive drunk who did not love her, who only saw her as a servant and occasional bed partner. Her time was not going to finish abruptly with a fistful of pills and a tumbler of bourbon, or a skull shattered trying to protect her children from their own father, or in any of the other dozens of horrible ways she had imagined.

He could see it in her eyes. Her days were going to end with her in a rocking chair next to her loving husband. She was going to have grandchildren because now she had a reason to live long enough to meet them. Holding out his arms to her, Sam lowered his head slightly, whispering, ''Oh, sweetheart—what have I done to you?''

Running across the room, Betty threw herself into her husband's arms. Pulling him as close as she could, squeezing him so tightly she hurt her own wrists, she answered, tears streaking her voice, ''You came back to me. That's all. You came back.''

Sam held the crying woman, comforting her with the words he now knew she wanted to hear. Moving her to the couch, he kissed her forehead, her eyes, her nose, her lips, telling her how good things were going to be from then on.

As he did he laughed inside his head, thinking two things.

I'm never going to hurt this woman ever again.

And I'm *glad* Al's not here.

CHAPTER
SIXTEEN

Sam sat in Mark Ralston's apartment, wondering at how he and the others were going to proceed. The night before had been filled with revelations for the people in their organization. Penzler, their man on the inside at Oregon Removal & Transport, had brought them everything they had ever wanted. More than they had ever wanted. Now their only problem was worrying over what to do about it.

Standing up, Sam paced the quiet room, drinking his third cup of coffee that day. He would have liked some music, but Ralston only had a small stereo system in his bedroom. He thought about turning it up loud enough so that it could be heard throughout the apartment, but only for a moment.

Wouldn't do to have it on like that when the others get here . . . not if it's not something Ralston wouldn't normally do. Can't get people started questioning him—

not fair to let him come back to a lot of confused friends.

At least we're finally on the track to getting out of here and actually letting the professor come back.

"Not my fault that I got here early, or that Al's *still* not here, or even that we had such a rough trip Leaping into here in the first place," he defended himself quietly. Or at least, I don't *think* it was my fault. Could I have done something that caused the bad Leap? And could that be why Al can't get through? God, I hope nothing has happened to him.

Sam sighed. Bypassing his comfortable leather chair once again, he went into the kitchen. Opening the refrigerator, he began pulling out an assortment of things for his soon-to-be-arriving guests.

"Hey, we had a bad ride, and now things are different than usual. Get over it. Stop worrying about how this Leap got started and just get on with doing your job."

Finally, the clock reached four—Klein and the others would be there any minute. Sam looked over the table in the dining area to see if there was anything he might add. He had set out two types of pickles, one dish of sweet, one sour. He had cut up a small block of cheddar cheese and half a mozzarella ball he had found, mixing the small cubes in a bowl. Then he had set the bowl on a plate and surrounded it with slices from a nearly intact pepperoni stick.

Celery and apples had been sliced up and mixed in one dish, raisins and dry roasted peanuts in another. Then he had taken all the candy he could find in the apartment . . . a third of a bag of M&M's, a handful of miniature peanut butter cups, several peppermint patties, and a cupful of mini-candy bars made by the Hershey people . . . thrown it all together in the same snack basket and set it within easy reach of the sofa.

By the time he got done filling the napkin holder, the front bell rang. He moved to the door quickly, opening it, admitting the people who thought they knew him. Dr. Klein took one look at the table, and then turned to stare at Sam.

"What is this?"

"It's food, Frank."

"I can see that," answered the doctor, reaching for a sour pickle, his other hand already filled with pepperoni and cheese. Turning to give his friend a teasing smile, he said, "I just wondered what it was doing *here.*"

"Ha . . . ha," answered Sam dryly.

He had not thought that with his multitude of sterling habits Ralston would turn out to be a bad host. But since several of the others made comments to match Klein's, such seemed the case. Trying to cover, Sam said that he thought he should do something special since they had so much to celebrate. The statement sent a chill through the air. Sensing he had said the wrong thing, he asked, "What? What's wrong?"

"We might not have as much to celebrate as we thought."

"Why?" asked Sam, perplexed.

Terri McCullen, one of the people he had met the night before at the meeting, a hardware store manager working on her masters degree, turned away from the snack table. Her lips were pressed tight together.

"A lot, Mark. One whole lot."

"What are you trying to tell me, Terri?" asked Sam.

Sadly, it made sense to him that something had gone wrong. After all, he was sure the environmentals' concerns were at the heart of his latest Leap. Last night's information should have solved all their problems. But he was still here, still Professor Mark Ralston, which meant there was still something for him to do. Before Terri could answer his question, however, Sam added, "And listen—if you're going to give me some bad news . . . link it up. Let's go over the whole history of this thing. Sometimes all you need to do is to hear something said out loud to make the answer you're looking for clear. I know this might sound unlikely, but . . ."

"No," interrupted Klein. "You're right. If we've got to start all over from scratch anyway . . . let's not beat around the bush about it. Let's just do it." The older man reached down for one of the paper plates Sam had put out and began to fill it, trying to keep a straight face as he added, "At least we won't be doing it on an empty stomach . . . like most of the times we come here."

Everyone settled in and began to go over their problem, filling in a few of the holes Sam had still had after their meeting of the night before. The tale of their informal group-with-no-name was a simple one. They did not engage in mass mailings, raising funds, disrupting licensed hunters during legal seasons, petitioning Congress, leading boycotts, chaining themselves to trees, protesting DDT, or going on hunger strikes in front of television cameras. Some of them might do such things individually, but it was not the purpose for which they had formed their group.

128

For the past five years they had been tracking the movements of known, major polluters, turning over what information they gathered to the proper government officials. They had been moderately successful, had achieved some good results. At least, they had until they had tried to take on Oregon Removal & Transport.

The company had picked up the contracts for seven of the ten worst violators on the group's list over the past half decade. And since then, none of the seven—or any of OR&T's other clients, for that matter—had been caught in any major transgressions. Several times the group had had information from people like Penzler on the inside. They had known—*for a fact*—that substances were going to be illegally dumped on this or that night. Barrels of spent copper-cleaning chemicals, or the poisonous "hot" water left over from reactor flushings, the reeking top-chum skimmed off vats of all manner of recycled products, all of it to be dumped on the open desert floor to rot and fester.

But every time they alerted someone, letting them know that corporation A was about to illegally dump a load of B, it would be pointed out that A had no B to dump. Which was followed by no little embarrassment for the officials acting on the group's information. Yes, it was true that the group had pointed the authorities to a great number of dump sites that had led to a number of arrests. But the people taken into custody had all been small fish, little independent truckers, sometimes just kids with a stolen pickup. The majority of those snared were reluctant to talk for the most part. Those who were not reluctant never had any actual facts to give up.

129

Now, even though the group had much more detailed information than ever before, thanks to Penzler, none of their contacts in high places would listen. Some of the people who might have believed them in the past were now in new positions, some had retired, still others were smarting from being burned by wrong information and simply did not trust them any longer.

The constant failure had taken its toll. The news that they could not get a single person at any kind of agency—environmental or simply even some all-purpose body like the state police or the sheriff's office—to take up their cause had severely disheartened them.

After all, the mood of the room seemed to cry, what's the use of trying if we can't get anything done.

And so, thought Sam, here at last is the real problem. The bad guys have been getting away with stuff for a long time. The good guys have the information that will put them away, and no one will believe them. And from the looks of them, they're getting ready to throw in the towel.

Sam slapped Mark Ralston's hands together and began rubbing his palms back and forth. As the others watched him, not exactly sure what to make of his actions, he leaned forward, smiling as he said, "So, fellow travelers, our old friends at Oregon R&T are going to take on some kind of nasty-type contract tomorrow night. Penzler doesn't know what it is, he just knows that it's bad news. All right, a few questions."

Klein sat forward, puzzled by Ralston's sudden animation. He had been perplexed by more than a few things his friend had done during the preceding few days, but he had eventually dismissed them. Well aware that no one follows the same order every day, especially people wound as tightly as Professor Mark Ralston, he had simply made note of the distraction his usually sharp friend had been exhibiting. Now, Klein felt, they were finally going to find out what had been distracting him.

"First off, and I want everyone to be as honest as they possibly can, because it could very well be important."

McCullen sat as far forward in her chair as Klein was in his. The others stirred as well, wondering what the professor could be up to. Having paused long enough to get the level of attention he desired, Sam asked, "Does everyone here trust Penzler?" When he saw several of their faces preparing to deliver standard answers, he added, "I mean it—would you really, *really* trust this man? With say your life, if necessary? I'm not saying I do or don't . . . I just want to get a consensus."

When the consensus finally rendered was that Penzler's information—like Penzler himself—was trustworthy, Sam accepted their judgment and moved on, asking, "Do we all really believe that what we've been told here is accurate? In other words, is Oregon Removal & Transport about to do something so heinous, so much worse than what they've done in the past, that they simply must be stopped?"

Beginning to see where Sam was heading, but not able to stop him—not really wanting to—the group agreed that from the level of disinformation Penzler had had to sift through to find what facts he had, that the company had to be up to something truly dire.

Over the past few years, the group had found dumps they knew were the sludge left from OR&T clients that had poisoned rivers, killed cattle, wildlife, and even a number of endangered animals. Their illegal activities had strangled more than one bald eagle, and even, the group suspected, several human beings. And none of what they had done in the past—if weighing the number of layers of cover-up used then against those used this time were any indication—could compete with what they were about to do.

"We pulled back on reporting our activities because we were worried about getting this kind of reaction. We were afraid that if we handed out one more wrong ticket that no one would ever help us again. Well, we were wrong. The last bad turn we gave out was the last straw . . . people were just too polite to tell us."

Sam looked at the men and women gathered with him. He was about to propel them into something—something big, possibly dangerous. It was not the kind of thing he generally did. He was supposed to be fixing glitches in time—not leading troops into battle . . . troops that might not have even been troops or known that there was a battle if not for him.

Are you sure about what you're doing here, Sam? Do you have the right to start something like this? Screw up people's lives just to make "something" come out right?

I'm the one God, Time, or Whoever chose for this job, he answered. There's *nothing* more important than making the Leap come out the way it's supposed to.

"Well, I say the only way we're going to get anything done here is to just up and do it ourselves."

Nothing.

CHAPTER
SEVENTEEN

"Give that to me," ordered Dr. Beeks. Al handed over the cupful of coffee. Even when he had been in the military, there had been no arguing with doctors.

"Wives, doctors, lawyers, accountants . . . they all belong to the same union," another admiral had told him once. "Just accept whatever they say and take it."

Al watched as Verbeena Beeks turned away from him, heading straight back to Sam. Her enthusiasm for the idea she had hatched was infectious. He knew that she was right, absolutely and positively knew it. Finally whoever was inside Sam Beckett's body was going to come out and say "hello." And Al wanted a ringside seat so he could dig into his bag of a million and one questions.

Beeks came alongside Sam's bed. Taking the cup, she slowly extended her hand toward his nose, saying, "So often, the Leapers coming here, they've been too frightened to come forward . . . some catatonic . . . it seemed so natural this time . . .''

She passed the cup under Sam's nose, moving it a few inches past his head, and then moved it back. All the time, she kept talking, telling Al, ''With all that happened to Ziggy, the complete breakdown on her conceptual functions, I kept thinking that what was wrong here was within Sam's mind. The brain is the greatest computer we know . . . and I was going down the wrong trail . . . thinking that what had happened to Ziggy was what had happened to Sam. But, now, I don't think so.''

The doctor responded with a smile to the reaction she was seeing on Sam's face. His eyes were blinking rapidly. Al came forward, crowding Beeks. She scolded him, pushing him off with one arm, careful not to spill any coffee on her patient. The admiral circled the bed, his eyes glued to Sam.

Pulling a cigar from his pocket, he stuck it into his mouth unlit, chewing on it with satisfaction and expectation. As he did, he and the doctor both watched Sam's body for further reactions.

''When you mentioned coffee before, you made me think. All the shots in the world weren't helping. So . . . what did we have to lose?''

Her hand kept moving back and forth at the same speed. With every pass the activity grew within Sam's face, his fingers.

''I don't know why I didn't try this before,'' said Beeks absently, ''I guess I was so busy thinking that this was a problem of his brain, something complicated . . .''

''Thinking of the kind of stuff that goes into fancy

research papers instead of your patient," added Al gruffly.

The doctor's face hardened, but she made no immediate comment. Part of her was ashamed to admit that the thought of being able to play in an arena where no other doctor in the history of the world had just might have blinded her to simpler answers . . . momentarily, anyway.

Putting aside the self-doubt for now, Verbeena continued waving the coffee under her patient's nose. "I had a professor once, couldn't form a coherent sentence without at least two cups of coffee in the morning. Swore that his mind needed it to function, and that without it he was catatonic. Used himself as an object lesson in addiction." She shrugged, as though to disavow any responsibility for such a crazy scheme. Then, suddenly, she cried, "Look! Look!"

"I've got eyes, Doctor," said Al, with a level, long-time military man's you-can't-impress-me tone. "I can see."

On the bed between them, Sam Beckett's eyes opened fully, staring about the room, completely focused.

"Can you hear me?" Al asked. Not waiting for an answer, he shouted, "Who are you?"

"Admiral!" Beeks said firmly, moving the hot coffee in her hand away from Sam's face. With her head high, straight, and defiant, she ordered, "Stop harassing my patient."

"The hell I will. Your patient is awake now—finally—and I want to know who he, she, or it is—what they know and what they don't."

"You'll get your information when I say you can."

Al pulled the cigar from his mouth and shouted, "I am not minutes overdue here. I am not hours overdue. I am *days* overdue. Do you understand the concept? *Days!* Your patient is not in that bed—your patient is lost in time, and whoever *is* in that bed is our only chance to save him!"

"Excuse me . . ." a weak voice interrupted. "But could somebody tell me just what's goin' on around here? And maybe get me some of that coffee I smell while they're at it?"

Al gestured that the doctor should give Sam the coffee. Beeks leaned over the restraining rail and held the cup to his lips. While whoever had woken up inside Sam sipped at the brew slowly, Al said, "You'll pardon me if I'm abrupt, but there is something serious happening here and I don't have any time to waste."

"Admiral," cautioned the doctor, "this is my area. You should not be in here. You might say something that the patient should not hear, that . . ."

"Doctor—right now there isn't anything going on in this Project that isn't my area. I'm responsible here, and I'd rather go down for saving Sam's ass in some unorthodox way than get off and cover my own by letting him down."

The speech was given in a tone calibrated to get across that the matter was closed. His eyes shifting from the doctor's face to Sam's, he started up again.

"You—whoever you are—are in no trouble. None whatsoever. There's a lot that has to be explained, but

137

that's going to have to come later. Right now, you have to tell me . . ."

Al took his handlink out of the hip pocket he had squeezed it into earlier. Stabbing at its buttons, he went too fast, getting two out of sequence. Cursing, he erased his error and started over. Lights flashed across his face, pink, green, yellow, pink, pink again, white . . .

"Who are you?"

"What?"

"I said," repeated Al, "who are you?"

"Who wants to know?" The man on the bed, obviously revitalized by the infusion of straight caffeine, was also obviously stubborn.

"You want to know who I am?" Al said with deadly calm. "I will tell you who I am. Admiral Albert Calavicci. I am in charge here and I am asking the questions."

"Navy," answered the still unidentified squatter in Sam's body. "Christ o'Petes, even worse than the Army. Don't know what I done gone and did now to get a big, bad sailor like you all mad at me, Admiral Popeye, sir, but I guess it ain't gonna hurt to tell ya my name."

Al raised the handlink again, using it to communicate with Ziggy. She could hear what went on in the Waiting Room, but they had found in the past that it was best not to have the walls in there "talk." She could work on the information as she got it, and guide Al's questions through the handlink.

Al knew already that Sam had Leaped into a man, and a hard case at that. He could tell that from the first few words. He had been dealing with that kind of stubbornness—in the military and out—too long not to know

138

what it sounded like. On the level of one man to another, he knew what kind of person was in the bed, and had acted as he thought best.

Now, he wasn't so sure. The man had been belligerent, nasty even. Until he tried to give his name. Then his face contorted as if speaking had somehow become horribly difficult. He stuttered, fumbling words so badly that they were unintelligible. The admiral held off asking any more questions, giving the man a moment to try again. He could read the frustration as well as the anger on Sam's face, and wondered what the hell was going on.

"Ralston. Ward Ralston." The man shouted the words, loudly, defiantly, as if speaking them were a challenge. Seconds after he did so, the handlink shifted colors. Looking down, Al could see that Ziggy was confirming the residency of a Ward Farrell Ralston in Portland, Oregon.

"Portland," mumbled Al. "That's not one of the two sites the Zig came up with before." Despair filled the admiral. Now what? Al prepared to ask the man identifying himself as Ward Ralston—the man staring out from Sam Beckett's eyes—another question.

Before he could, however, the man said, "I don't think he cares."

Beeks and the admiral both stared. As they watched, Ward continued to carry on a conversation, but not with either of them. Talking to someone else that was in the room whom they could not see, he asked, "And what makes you think that?"

The pause lasted several seconds, after which Ward

said, "No, I don't think so. I think you don't get to say shit here."

Out of the corner of his mouth, Al whispered to the doctor, "What is going on here? Has anyone that ever landed here before acted like this?"

"Not once," she answered, telling him, "to be honest, I was about to ask you what you thought."

"No way, Mark—hell with you. I ain't been wrestlin' with you for all this time just to give up now. Un-uh. No way. Get yourself your own . . ."

Al's conscious mind stopped listening to the babble coming out of Sam, trying to make heads or tails out of any of it. He could see from the look on Beeks's face, by the way she was standing, her hands moving slightly, hesitantly, that she was as confused as he was.

Now what? he wondered, feeling tired, out of sorts, and even a bit out of his league. Oh, God—now what?

The lights on his handlink shifted. Al stared down, watching the information appear on the miniature screen. Ziggy had taken the one bit of solid information that had come through Ward Ralston's rambling monologue and done as much as she could.

"Mark," said Al, feeling slow for having missed it when it had been said, fascinated to see where it went. "Mark Thornton Ralston. Reno, Nevada."

The other destination, thought Al, his mind boggling. There are two people—there is a Ward Ralston and there is a Mark Ralston. One lives behind Door Number Two. And the other—the handlink shifted colors again—is a long-distance trucker.

As the doctor stared at him, Al suddenly started to

laugh. He finally understood.

So simple, he thought, his mind retreating from the implications of what he had just figured out. Practically reeling from the weight of his discovery, he turned to the doctor.

"Twins, Verbeena." When she only blinked, he told her softly, trying to understand it himself, "Sam's Leaped into twins."

CHAPTER
EIGHTEEN

Sam was on the road again. He was behind the wheel of his rig, aimed down a long, straight draw of desert blacktop. He had his Jack's Gun Shop cap on, a cigarette in his mouth, and a full thermos on the seat next to him. Ward smoked, so he had to, as well. He didn't think he had ever smoked in his own personal life, but now . . . well, he told himself, now was different.

He felt at ease behind the big wheel. He felt at ease with being Ward Ralston, period. All of his years as Sam Beckett, he had never felt as free as he did at this moment.

No more responsibilities, no more worries, no more cares, he thought. That's me. Then, after a moment's quiet reflection watching the desert fly by on both sides, he amended his rash list, thinking, Well, all right, there are still a few responsibilities. And probably even a few worries and cares. But not like back in

1999, or . . . whatever year it was now.

Coming to an incline, Sam downshifted, pressuring the gas pedal at the same time, saying, "Who cares? Who gives a damn, anyway? Not me, brother. Not anymore."

Sam meant it. As far as he was concerned Leaping had become a thing of the past. The cosmos had finished with him and he had been given his reward. Being Dr. Sam Beckett had been a dead-end proposition—a workaholic dweeb without the good sense to stop and, as people were wont to say, get a life.

"Well, that's over."

Before he had hit the road this time, Sam had gotten together with Betty and gone over all of their finances. They had dug out the bank books, the checking file, their credit cards, and mortgages. Ward had been surprisingly organized about keeping their records, but he had never allowed Betty to touch any of it. Sam "admitted" that that was just another one of "his" mistakes. They sat up the entire night, seeing what they had in the way of bills and assets.

By morning they had it all clear and discovered they were not nearly as bad off as Betty had thought. They celebrated by splurging and cooking an entire pound of bacon just for themselves while the kids were still asleep. Betty cut slices from one of her homemade loaves while Sam tended to the bacon. As it cooked, she got out the plates, the lettuce, the tomatoes, the mayonnaise, and some flatware. And while she took care of all that, Sam chopped up a large onion and then sprinkled the thin slivers across the frying bacon.

"What are you doing?" asked Betty, not so much surprised at the thought of onions on bacon, but at the sight of her husband doing anything so creative.

"I'm experimenting."

"Un-huh," she said, half-asleep, teasing. "Who are you all of a sudden? Dr. Frankenstein?"

"I don't want to have to get all the neighbors and chase it through the street with torches . . . I just want to eat it."

"Oh, Ward," she said, whispering so as not to break the magical atmosphere. "I don't know what's happened to you. I don't know what's brought you back to me . . . but, I just have to tell you . . . I am so happy. Whatever it is, it's the best thing in the whole world."

"I understand, sweetheart," he said, smiling at her, stirring his bacon and onions around in an endless circle. She came and hugged him around the waist, pulling him into herself, touching him just simply so she could feel him again, as if he had been away from her for years.

"Ward, oh, my baby," she said, hugging him tighter. "You don't even talk the same anymore."

"Is that a bad thing?" Sam tried to keep from tensing. He was trying to keep his own formidable vocabulary in check, but he could not abide hearing Ward's dropped Gs, or the constant stream of "yer" and "ain't" and the like that made up his former host's limited speech patterns.

After all, if I'm staying here, it's on my terms. The cosmos didn't give me this guy so I could talk like Deputy Dawg the rest of my life.

"Oh, no," Betty told him, her voice filled with a re-

144

assuring tone of honesty. "It sounds so fine. I don't know how you did it. It wasn't even me that noticed it, right off."

"Well, if it wasn't you," asked Sam, slightly perplexed, "who was it?"

"It was Taylor. He mentioned it yesterday before you got back." Sam wondered what the boy's reason had been for pointing out the change. But, before he could ask, Betty told him, "You won't believe it. He was just going on and on, talking about all the things that seem different about you. All sorts of little things that must have been flying right by me."

Releasing her hold on his waist, Betty slid her arms up her husband's chest, bringing her fingers up over his shoulders, touching his back. Putting her head against his neck, she hugged him again, telling him, "He's so very proud of you."

"Well," said Sam, paying more attention to his cooking than what he was saying, "a boy's got to have someone to look up to. I couldn't go around being a bum forever, could I?"

When Betty did not answer, Sam asked again, "Could I?"

He felt the tear rolling down his neck. Switching off the stove, he set down his utensil and took Betty's hands in his, breaking her embrace so he could turn her around and look at her.

"Hey now, little girl," he said softly, with more love in his voice than she had heard in her entire life, "what'd I do, now? You know I've been putting a lot of effort into not making you cry anymore."

145

She buried her face in his chest then, kissing him and whispering his name over and over. He held her and kissed her and before long found himself crying. In that instant Sam Beckett hated Ward Ralston for many things. For the way he had treated his wife and his children. For the way he had wasted his life. For simply not knowing what he had while he still had it.

And if he had thought Ward did not deserve his life back before, he was convinced then. Tapping Betty gently on the back, he tugged at her, saying, "Come on, sweetheart. I didn't cook up that mess of bacon for nothing."

"Okay," she said, laughing, "now I know the fairies didn't come down and switch my real husband for some changeling." When he simply stared at her, she said, "You may have made some powerful changes in yourself . . . but mealtime is still the ultimate experience. Right?"

"Oh, you are so correct, honey lamb," he answered, carrying the oversize, burnt steel skillet to the table. Placing it on the large black iron trivet in the center of the table, he said, "Now, you ready for breakfast?"

Betty slid into her chair, reaching for two slices of bread, telling him, "I'm ready to ride a passenger seat into hell if you're sitting in the driver's seat."

After that they had stuffed themselves with fat sandwiches, both dripping with tomato juice and bacon fat. Like kids, they had both made their sandwiches as large as they could, piling on the mayonnaise, layering lettuce and extra slices of bread until neither of them could hold what they had built with one hand. And, after that, there

146

had been no choice but to hoist their creations with both hands and smash them into their faces, taking exaggerated bites that left their faces sloppy with grease and crumbs.

They laughed the entire time, and then they left the kitchen a wreck, going back to the bedroom. Sam slurped a spot of mayo off Betty's nose; she pulled a shred of lettuce out of his hair and ate it. He tasted the side of her face, licking crumbs away as he went. And then he found her mouth, and they fell into each other, staying there until Sam had to head out for his big money run, the one that was going to straighten out all their problems once and for all.

Thinking about the morning behind him only made Sam smile. Deep down in his heart, he knew he was doing the right thing. He had fixed every problem in Ward Ralston's life, and yet he had not Leaped.

"And," he said, slapping out a tune on his dashboard as he sped through the desert at close to 100 mph, "I'm not going to, either. I can stop worrying about getting plucked out of here, because this Leap's going to last a lifetime. Proof's in the pudding. I Leap to fix lives. But the only thing wrong with Ward Ralston's life . . . was . . . Ward Ralston. So . . ."

He pulled the chord to the air horn, letting out a tremendous long blast of sound that echoed across the desert.

"Bye, bye, Ward Ralston."

The horn bellowed again, loud and blaring, a noise loud enough to dispel fog or shatter glass.

"Bye, bye. And everyone's life is better."

Sam stepped on the gas, urging the eighteen-wheeler to even greater speed as he followed the straight line of road away into the distance.

CHAPTER
NINETEEN

"You know, Mark," said Klein as the two crossed the parking lot, "I do believe we just might be able to do this." He made his statement with a faraway, absent kind of voice that seemed to imply that he had made his decision after some extended period of doubt.

Chuckling, Sam told him, "Your faith in our abilities overwhelms me, Herr Dok'tor."

"Funny boy," answered the shorter man. "Quite a wit you have there. You'll go far. I predict it."

"Well, be all that as it may," said Sam as he shoved the proper key into the door of Mark Ralston's minibus, "you still sounded a little doubtful there."

Opening the door, he pressed the button that electronically unlocked all the other doors so that the two of them could store the bundles they had been carrying in the back seat. Then they clambered into the front seat.

After they were secured inside the car and confident

they had everything, Sam keyed the ignition and moved them out and on their way. Once out on the road, he swung the conversation around, returning to what he had been saying just before they got into the car.

"You are comfortable with what we're doing here, aren't you, Frank?"

"Yes, certainly," answered the older man. "It's just an idea that takes a little getting used to."

"Why's that?" asked Sam politely.

"I'm older than you are, Mark. Mentally as well as chronologically. You're more a part of the electronic age than I am. This playing at . . . what should I call it? I know none of us is going to suddenly start acting like James Bond or something, but still, breaking up into teams and going out to hide at the different possible dump sites . . . taking video cameras . . . it's not the kind . . ."

As Klein talked, Sam thought about things from his standpoint, one the doctor could not share. He was willing to push things more than a regular person might because, of course, he was not a regular person. He was not even the person Klein thought he was.

I'm also getting more used to doing things like this. Every time I Leap into someone, they end up doing things they normally wouldn't do. I'm sure, no matter how swell everyone thinks Ralston is, that he never would have suggested what we're doing. That's why I Leap here and there in the first place.

Often in the past he had wondered what happened to people after he Leaped on to his next assignment. He had made heroes of so many people in so many different ways, turned so many ordinary, regular folk into risk-takers—what happened to them the next time someone expected them to act like a man with a mission, or a woman with unbelievable powers of insight, or a child with boundless courage? What happened the next time in their lives someone thought they could count on the person he had been to be that person again . . . and they were only themselves? Were they pushed into situations they couldn't handle? Or did they rise to the test even as Sam had, coming through as heroes once again?

This time, he was surprised to find that he no longer seemed to care.

Maybe, he thought, I've just been Leaping so long I've gotten a little indifferent. Or maybe it doesn't matter as much as I thought. After all, how many of the people I've Leaped into would have preferred I didn't? My personal choices don't mean anything, why should theirs? We do what we have to, and move on. That's all.

Sam's eyes darted from sign to sign, trying to spot the right road. He had suffered this problem before, of being in the role of someone who was supposed to know where he was, trying to drive someone else to a place he had never heard of. There was only so much he could learn from memorizing road maps. Maps didn't list little back streets. They didn't tell you what roads had construction on them which every local resident knew had to be avoided. They also dealt in approximations—an inch equals seventy-five miles—hard to decide how many blocks equaled eight tenths of an inch.

He couldn't worry about it overmuch, however. He continued to nod at the appropriate moments as he listened to Klein with half an ear, while his thoughts ran on their own way.

If all the people I've Leaped into had the facts—if they could see what the results would have been if I hadn't been there to take a hand in things, how many of them would call for a recount? How many marriages have I saved—how many lives? How many? And that's just the surface. All those people I've put back together with each other . . . who can say who their children are going to be? Al and Ziggy can only tell me the history that we've effected up to the point where they know what history is—they've only got *their* latest information.

Spotting the exit sign leading onto 395 South, Sam swung the bus easily onto the ramp. As they moved down the grade from the street-level traffic into the flow moving out of town, Klein unfolded a road map. He whistled again at the distance they would be covering, commenting on how exciting it was to be doing something so . . . "crazy." Canceling their classes, leaving everyone in the lurch for two days while they ran off to try to catch the bad guys . . . "crazy."

Sam smiled silently, knowingly. Only crazy to someone who did not have his special perspective. Sam speculated on how much good he had done. He thought of the children to come, again.

Those children who would be born after he Leaped out of a situation, because of something he had done— how many of them would grow up to do important things? Cure cancer—fly to Mars—solve the population problem—cure the problem of ocean damage from oil spills and industrial drainage—

Or even just be happy? If I just keep Leaping for no other reason than to give the world hundreds of happy people, people who don't hate each other, murder each other . . . who don't cheat or steal or rape, or even just don't manipulate each other. Even that would be good enough.

"So . . . you're letting me do all the talking," said Klein. Sam almost resented being drawn back from his mental wanderings.

"You weren't saying anything I disagreed with. Why should I butt in?"

"I know everybody thinks I love the sound of my own voice, and . . . it's true. It's a beautiful voice and I do love the sound of it. But I have been going on and on about the pros and cons of what we're doing here. Driving hundreds of miles so we can sit in the desert to try and spot illegal dumpers and catch them on videotape. Don't you have any comeback?"

"Well," Sam answered, not able to stop smiling as he did so, still basking in the warm memory of all the good he figured he had done, "I guess I like the idea of putting on a suit of armor and riding off to do battle with the bad guys. I mean, everyone wants to be a hero—deep down."

"We all want to do the right thing," Klein agreed seriously. "Whatever we believe that right thing to be. And being a hero *is* a nice fantasy—I won't try and turn aside a hundred years of psychological research just for the sake of argument. But still, if we do this, and we

153

catch these people, and say we even don't get caught up in court trials and the such . . .''

Klein paused for such a long time that Sam finally had to nudge him, asking, ''Yesssss?''

''I'm sorry. You're so gung ho about this you almost make me ashamed. But I am a bit worried. People committing crimes tend to be more dangerous than your average university personnel. And that's what we are. Even if we take the limelight today—even if, I'll reach for the absurd for a moment—we were to become celebrities of the *60 Minutes* variety—tomorrow we'll still be your average university personnel.''

Sam narrowed his eyes for a moment, biting at his lower lip. Not quite knowing how to answer Mark Ralston's colleague, he chose a question instead, throwing the ball back into the older man's court with a simple, ''What are you getting at, Frank?''

''I mean . . . and I hate to sound as if I'm putting simple self-interest ahead of social responsibility, especially since that's exactly what I'm doing . . . but, I'm saying that even if we don't get shot in the back of the head and dumped in a shallow ditch—''

''Frank.''

''I'm in the realm of sweeping generalities here. Please allow me my moment.'' Klein set down the map he had been holding throughout their conversation. Using both his hands to illustrate his points, he started waving them in an animated fashion, saying, ''If I expected to be murdered I would not be here, I would be home watching CNN to see who was murdered. But we *could* be killed. We could catch some very frustratingly evil people in the act and maybe stir up enough muck to cause them a small amount of trouble—which may or may not cause them to retaliate against us in some manner—we may end up television hacks bouncing from show to show to grab a few dollars and self-promote the book we'll write on saving the environment which some shill will come out of the woodwork for if we're deemed hot enough. We may end up with nothing more than wasted time on our hands.''

The doctor dropped his hands in his lap then. He took a deep breath, and then began talking once more in a less excited tone.

''Whatever the case, when it is all over we will both return to being simple university personnel. I will. At least, I hope I will. To me, 'hero' is a temporary state. There is no Superman, Mark.''

''And your point, Frank?''

Klein pressed his upper lip against his teeth. He knew what he wanted to say, he just did not know how to treat a colleague he respected as deeply as he did Mark Ralston as a patient. Summoning up the objectivity every doctor needed, however, he steeled his feelings away, and answered the question.

''I'm not so sure about you, though.'' After Sam expressed a degree of surprise on Mark Ralston's behalf, the older man said, ''I'm not trying to put you on the spot or get you to turn the van around. I'm just giving you a cautionary sounding. If I didn't know you better, I'd swear you were suffering from some sort of quixotic fixation. Now, it's nothing overt, but—and it's a large relief to just say this and get it out of my head—I've

155

been catching little turns of phrase, little glints in your eyes . . . maybe you're just very caught up in all of this at the moment, we have been trying to get something on these people for a long time . . .''

Klein allowed his words to trail off. He was uncomfortable with the subject, not sure how he could be saying what he was to a friend, to a man he had known as long as he had Mark Ralston. Such things did not develop in a person's makeup overnight. It was impossible. And yet, if he had not known the man behind the driver's wheel as long as he had . . .

''Anyway,'' he added, throwing as much distance between himself and any ugly intent his friend might have been able to find in what he was saying, ''I don't know. Perhaps it's just that since I feel that I'm much more worried about the ramifications of this than you are— than I expect you to be—that I'm projecting a wrong thinking attitude onto you to keep myself from feeling embarrassed.''

I'm impressed, thought Sam, feeling a bit foolish for having been so clearly spotted. If it weren't for the fact that nobody's very likely to figure out that a man from the future is Leaping into other people at the direction of either fate or a very expensive computer, this guy's come as close to the truth as any that have tried.

Sam lifted one of his hands from the steering wheel, waved it about in a small circle, and answered in as light a voice as he could muster, ''Well, of course, how do I respond to that? If I get upset or defensive, you'll figure that I am disturbed. But if I try to reassure you and just brush it off, you'll still figure I'm disturbed. It's the

156

beauty of our profession, but it is a bit of a Catch-22.''

"I understand," answered Klein, grateful to have gotten his concern off his chest. "I do. I don't know what was bothering me, really. Maybe I've been watching too many bad sci-fi movies. Anyway"—the doctor slapped his knees with finality—"I got the notion in my head that you weren't acting like yourself, and I blew it up into a full basket of the jitters. Can you forgive me?"

"I think I can," said Sam, grateful to be out from under the microscope.

He had forgotten, even while he had been thinking about what happened to people after he Leaped out of them, that sometimes the people around him took note of his host while he was there. As he and Klein continued along their long drive, chatting about far more mundane matters, he thought to himself.

It's interesting that even though the doctor did spot me, the only change he saw in Mark Ralston was that he had become more heroic. Will he still have that perception of Ralston when I'm gone, or will it be a momentary aberration under stress?

Dr. Sam Beckett had more than enough background to know exactly what Frank Klein had been trying to say. If he had been capable of really analyzing what was happening at that moment, he would have been far more worried than Dr. Klein.

CHAPTER
TWENTY

Ward Ralston's rig pulled up at the number seven loading dock at Oregon Removal & Transport's Bakersfield storage center in southern California. Sam had miscalculated his time somewhat, and had been forced to go without breaks to keep his schedule. Now, after a long number of unbroken hours, pushing to make it to the center by his appointed pickup time of 6:30, he could relax for a while before heading out again.

No worse than any of the all-nighters I pulled as Dr. Sam Beckett, he thought with grim satisfaction, arching his back and hearing it pop in several places. He thought about getting out and going for another cup of coffee to add to the thermos he'd had on the trip, but decided that what he really needed to find was the bathroom. That was the worst thing about this job, he thought as he climbed down from his cab and went in search of the facilities before presenting himself to whoever would supervise the actual loading of his truck. There wasn't much chance to stretch your legs and take care of life's little essentials. Other than that, assuming he got to go home more often than Ward had in the past, he didn't suppose it was such a bad job after all. In fact, there was something to be said for the "road warrior" mythos. Sam had spent a number of hours behind the wheel imagining himself as a modern cowboy, one of the last hard-riding traveling men, a proud member of a dying breed, and other clichés that embarrassed him almost as much as they pleased him.

The one thing that bothered him slightly through those self-pleased musings was the fact he had no ambivalence about his decision. He had debated taking Ward Ralston's life for a while, but not very vigorously. In a cold, matter-of-fact way, he did understand that it was not right for him to want to steal another man's life. No matter what kind of case could be made against Ward Ralston, the forces in the universe that had set Sam the task of "putting right what once went wrong" had nowhere along the line bestowed upon him the rank of judge, jury, or prosecutor.

But despite the number of times he realized that he now seemed quite comfortable doing certain things that a week earlier would have horrified him, he could not work up any concern. Nothing in him screamed out to stop. Nothing within him even seemed to want to suggest such a thing. For some reason he could not discern, Sam Beckett's conscience had decided to go on holiday.

Which, he thought, waiting for someone from inside the center to respond to his knock, is nonsense. Your conscience doesn't just walk out on you—it can't. All you can do is change your mind.

The sound of boot heels moving slowly over tile came to Sam from the other side of the door. He dropped his fist that was poised to knock again, taking on a hey-I'm-cool attitude.

As he stepped back to keep from being hit by the door when it opened, he thought, And that's all there is to it, I guess. I've changed my mind. I've done my part . . . more than my part. Let someone else run around doing drywall work on the last four decades—a memory of Betty's face flashed through his mind—I've got better things to do.

The door opened. Sam was greeted by a man with the name "Mike" embroidered on his lapel.

"Merciful God in heaven," said the old man with a one-sided grin plastered to his face. "I guess they'll let just about any pile of flesh that can monkey a license outta the state drive a truck these days."

"Thanks, Mike," answered Sam, trying a neutral answer he hoped could be taken as surly or friendly. "I've got a big bag of respect for you, too."

The older man was at least sixty, short and dark-complected, sporting the kind of stubble that shouted out that, yes, he had indeed shaved that morning, but that his was not the kind of beard to take defeat lightly. Sam finished trading greetings with Mike, discovering that the two of them apparently were friends. After a few back slaps apiece, Mike finally insisted they "get the show on the road." Sam obliged willingly, following the older man down the brightly lit corridor into the holding office.

At Mike's instruction he surrendered his keys to a much younger man who was obviously waiting for them. Together, Sam and the supervisor went over the manifest for his delivery while the young dock hauler went out to move Sam's rig around the building to where the loaders could fill his trailer. He and Mike traded stories for a while, filling up on coffee and lies until the younger man returned.

"All set, Ward."

"Filled to the brim?" asked Sam.

The dock hauler slapped his knee for effect, changing over to a thick redneck accent as he answered, "Golllllllly, oh, yes, sir. Yes, indeed. With the finest brand of rotten, contaminated slop America's merchant class knows how to churn out."

"It's all tight-canistered, right?" asked Sam, joking but wanting to hear the answer. "You're not planning on turning my trailer into something that glows in the dark now, are you?"

"I screwed each screw myself," answered the younger man, not visibly annoyed in any way Sam could tell.

"Glad to hear it," he told the dock hauler. Turning to Mike, he asked, "And where's this load of goop get dropped?"

"All in the paperwork, you road pig. Now get your ass haulin' highway. I got two other guys waitin' and ten more due before midnight."

The three shook hands, swapped one last set of lies, and then with his keys returned and his new manifest,

Sam finally headed back down the same hallway from which he had entered. Outside, he found his rig returned to where he had left it originally. He could tell from the way the trailer was laying lower toward the wheels that it was most likely as full as it could be packed.

He stopped for a moment under one of the holding area's pole lights to read over the paperwork Mike had given him. Ward might know what was going on inside and out, but Sam was still new at living his life for him. He discovered that he had taken on a cargo of some ninety-eight barrels of sludge that had come from Bakersfield Alkaline Processors. Apparently they had conducted a legal scrubbing of their main foundry vats and had commissioned the southern California branch of OR&T to remove the residue for them.

Sam was to take his load to the OR&T holding storage dump center in the Rockies. Folding up his manifest, he slid the papers into his pocket and then threw his foot up on the wheel step to his cab. As he pulled himself up, using the door handle for a handgrip, he shook his head in amazement.

"I don't know why this job pays so much, but then, I don't care, either."

"Do tell," came a voice from inside his cab. Sam's head came level with the window of his door before he could stop himself. As he looked inside his cab, he found two men inside waiting for him. The man closest to the door smiled and said, "We'd be happy to talk to the boss and see if he couldn't see his way clear to cutting your fee, Ward."

Sam looked at the men's faces. They were hard and cold,

the faces of killers. The badly concealed bulges under their light jackets did nothing to dispel the image, either.

"Come on, Ward. Get in. We ain't got all night."

His mind racing, Sam thought, They know me—Ward—they're expecting me. This is all normal. This supposed to be happening. And if I don't go along with it, they're going to know something is up.

Pulling the door open, Sam used Ward Ralston's wide, clean smile to good effect.

"Hell, yes," he agreed, grateful to have Ward's supposed simplicity to hide behind. "Don't I know it."

Keying the ignition, hoping he could play his unexpected new hand, Sam said, "Well, on to the Rockies."

"What?" asked the man against the door, the one more in the shadows who could not be seen too clearly.

Sam explained, "The storage dump center in Idaho. That's where we're headed—right?"

Both men laughed. The one in the center turned to the other, asking him, "Didn't I tell you this guy was a card?" Handing Sam a beer, he said, "Come on, Ward. Let's do it. Like I said, we ain't got all night."

"So you did," agreed Sam, gunning the motor of Ward Ralston's truck. "So you did."

Following the directions given by the man in the center of the cab, Sam moved the rig out onto the highway, wondering what the hell that idiot Ward had gotten them into.

And, having watched the proceedings at the facility all evening through their binoculars, certain they had the right vehicle, Sam and his accomplice Dr. Frank Klein swung out into traffic, trailing the rig off into the night.

CHAPTER
TWENTY-ONE

"Listen, all I want to know is if you two have your act together or not, yet. And, to be perfectly honest, I would like to know sometime real soon."

Al Calavicci was not a happy man. Once Verbeena's inspiration had focused the twins' attention, it should have been a simple enough matter to get this Leap rolling again. But there was a hitch. Of course there was, he thought sourly. There was always a hitch. It just seemed that this Leap had more than its share. Double your pleasure, he snorted to himself. Double your fun. Hah. It had been less work *dating* twins—without them knowing—than getting these two to talk.

Mopping at his forehead, he found himself sweating despite the Project's perfectly maintained climate level of sixty-eight degrees. Growling to himself, he said, "This one takes the cake, Sam. I thought I'd seen a lot since all this started, but this has got to be the strangest yet. But you hang in there, pal. Hopefully you're having better luck wherever you are!''

The Ralston brothers were not the only people steaming Al at that moment. As his assistant interrogator, Verbeena Beeks had not been much help. Not as much as Al wished she would be, anyway. With the resistance he was getting from the Ralstons, the admiral's last suggestion to the doctor had been for her to use drugs of some kind so he could force the level of cooperation he needed from the pair. She had been shocked—he had not cared. She refused his request—he made it an order. She refused again, threatening charges—he reminded her of who had the ultimate authority and demanded cooperation. So far, she had been able to resist by offering alternatives, and by halfway convincing him that it wouldn't work anyway.

Al looked over at Beeks. As far as he was concerned, the doctor was running out of alternatives. She was sitting in the corner of the Waiting Room, watching him back—not hindering him at the moment, but offering no assistance, either. In truth, she *had* run out of alternate solutions and now simply did not know what to do next. She *did* know that drugs were not going to help any. Not without pushing Sam Beckett's body too far, and neither of them was willing to risk that.

Before they had to argue the point any further, however, they suddenly received help from an unexpected source—the Ralstons. Sam's body leaned forward, its mouth moving. For a moment, no sound came out.

Beeks stood up, still staring, wondering what exactly was happening. Seeing her attention shift to the bed, Al

165

turned back to her patient, noting what she was observing. Quickly he asked, "What's the story? Who've I got here?"

"Ma-Ma-Mark," the body stuttered.

"Oh, hi, Mark," answered Al sarcastically. He stared in weary exasperation, wondering how much longer he could control himself.

Al *did* know that if the pair of Leapers in Sam's body gave him any more trouble, he would do something he would regret. He closed his eyes, and just before he spoke, he made a silent prayer to God. Time. Or Whoever. Make something happen here, will you? Let's get this mess over with. Please.

And then, he asked, "So . . . what can I do for you, Mark?"

"I—I think Ward and I can help you now."

"Oh, you do, do you?" answered Al. "And how do you think you can do that?"

"We've been talking. Inside . . . here. Wherever we are. Which is good—right?"

Al stared at Sam's face. Wondering what information the twins were really seeking, he responded noncommittally. "Why are you asking me?"

"Because, ah, we thought that was what you wanted. I mean, somehow you brought us both here—put us in here together—in a body that won't move, can't walk or talk or . . . or anything, unless we cooperate with each other. Like some kind of therapy. All right—it worked."

Al stared. He could not think of anything else to do.

Dr. Beeks moved up alongside of him. She had far more experience with the Leapers who came to wait out their time in Sam's body. It was her main job to watch over them—to care for their mental health as well as Sam's physical well-being.

But twins . . . no one had ever imagined such a thing would happen. That it *could* happen. And certainly not twins who didn't seem to be able to stand each other. No one had ever prepared her for such an occurrence.

Damn you, Verbeena, she swore. No one prepared you for any of this. No one. None of it. Tough. You've written the whole book, well now it's time for a new chapter.

She turned away from Al, from the body on the bed, staring at the far wall of the Waiting Room. The admiral was not the only one at the Project who was tired. He was not the only one who had been pushed to the edge by this Leap, by the unprecedented strangeness it had brought with it. So stop trying to baby yourself and get back to work. You've got three patients now, and there isn't anybody who can do the job but you.

Verbeena knew she was right. Knew that if she let the silence hang any longer that the admiral would fill the void. Al Calavicci was a good man. He worked hard and she knew he would give his life for Dr. Beckett in an instant. But despite all his many accomplishments, he did not know much about clinical psychology.

Turning back around, the doctor offered a deal.

"We'll tell you when things have worked. So far, all we have out here is a wasted week. Why don't you get down to telling *us* what's been going on in there."

"Not much to tell, I reckon." Both Al and Verbeena were certain that it was no longer Mark Ralston who was speaking. As they listened, Ward said, "I mean, I

167

guess after a week of being piled on top of each other like this, even the two of us can learn to get along. A little, anyway.''

"And why is that so hard for you?"

"Hell, where would I start? We ain't said 'boo' to each other in fifteen years. Had to go through a lotta bad water to get even this far. Our folks split up, split us up, too. My dad got me, and Mark got our mother, and the snotty bastard she married. An antiques dealer.'' He made a face, expressing his disgust eloquently. "They sent Mark to private school, wouldn't let him dirty himself with the riffraff, which included his brother. Hell, we ain't even seen each other since our old man drank himself into the grave.''

"All right," said Al. His hands waving, he cut forward through the conversation, saying, "So, you've been having a great little confab for the past week. Great. You got all your problems worked out now?''

Verbeena shot him a look.

"Enough so that we can proceed with whatever it is that is happening to us here.''

Mark again. Damn, thought Al. This is going to get confusing.

"Okay, we'll proceed.''

"Admiral . . .''

"Doctor," Al said. "This is no time to play. You think I'm about to go where I shouldn't, you speak up. Right now, I have to get down to business.''

The doctor looked at her hands in frustration. She wanted to take control of the situation because the Waiting Room was supposed to be her ballpark. But Al could get answers faster than she could, and right now, in a different time, Sam Beckett needed those answers. And Sam was her patient, too, as much or more than the two deeply unnerved men residing in his body. She couldn't begin to imagine the strain Sam must be undergoing.

Project Quantum Leap had proved the moment Sam Beckett had stepped into the Accelerator that no one person could exist simultaneously with themselves in the same instance of time. And that meant . . . what? How could one mind, one personality . . . how did one individual manipulate two different human beings—live two lives?

Knowing what had to be done, for Sam's sake, but not liking it a bit, she narrowed her eyes into a scowl and nodded.

Al understood—taking the signal from Beeks to proceed, but to be cautious. He smiled slightly, a silent clue to let her know that he would. He knew she was under as much pressure as he was—maybe more. The admiral respected the doctor's talent, suspecting that she had already realized Sam's Leaping into twins caused a time paradox they had not had to deal with before.

Earlier, Al had left the Waiting Room briefly to ask Ziggy what possible effects this new Leap might have on Sam. The computer had fed him a list of eighty-seven different ways in which Sam's personality might unfold to accommodate the new Leap.

"Ultimately," Ziggy had answered, "it will depend on the personalities of the twins." When Al had demanded further explanation, the computer had obliged, telling him, "We know that the people Dr. Beckett Leaps into leave behind traces of themselves. Motor response, familiar ways of handling objects, the way they butter their toast, and so on. While Dr. Beckett concentrates on why he is there, much of the stored knowledge of their brains continue the day-to-day operations of their lives."

Ziggy continued her lecture, explaining far too many points in too fine a detail. When the admiral balked, begging that at least some of the answers be given in English, the computer told him, "Think of the brains of the individuals Dr. Beckett Leaps into as being like myself." When Al continued to stare, the female voice explained, "Think of them as computers. The information that controls their everyday functions is stored like programs in their brain's hard drive. Dr. Beckett does not have to access this information. It is part of the governing program and thus is accessed automatically whenever it is needed."

Ziggy paused for a moment for no apparent reason, then continued, picking up where she had left off.

"Dr. Beckett is like a disc-held program. To insert him into the computer, the program being run at the moment must be removed. It is removed, and Dr. Beckett is installed. He becomes the program one sees operating on-screen. Removing the other operational program does not disconnect the hard drive—it merely accesses the main drive's stored support programs in a different manner."

At that point, Ziggy paused again for another much longer moment. Then, with a flurrying flash of lights Al suspected was nothing more than unnecessary theatrics, the machine continued, saying, "This time, however, one disc is being asked to operate two computers. I can not think of any answer but to say that the support programs will have to take over more of the functions than they generally have to handle whenever Dr. Beckett Leaps."

"But that doesn't make any sense," said Al. "You can dupe a disc over and over. Why can't Sam just copy himself and Leap into ten people if he has to?"

Ziggy paused again. Al stared at the spot on the control panel he thought of as Ziggy's face through his right eye, his left closing slowly as he waited. Then finally, just before his left eye shut completely, the computer answered him, saying, "I am, as you are so fond of pointing out, a mere construct, Admiral Calavicci. And this being the case, while it is true that I was built to hold a certain ability to extrapolate information on my own, I was not actually built to form and maintain opinions of my own."

Al snorted. Ziggy often made speeches similar to the one she was feeding him when she was unsure of her ground. Drumming his fingers on the elbows of his folded arms, Al waited for the computer to get to the point.

"However," she said at last, "since this is an extraordinary moment, I will offer a theory. We do not know exactly what part of the individual Leapers it is that moves through time whenever they Leap. It has been postulated, many times by different people, several times by yourself . . ."

"Stop stalling, Zig," demanded Al. "Whatever it is you want to say, just spit it out."

"The soul—or the psyche, if you prefer—is not a computer disc."

"What?" Al had been surprised. Shaking his head as if he had not heard right, he asked, "What was that?"

"If whatever part of the human makeup constitutes the soul is the part of a person that Leaps, then I do not think it can be duplicated by any simple means. The soul is the sum of one person's life—it cannot be duplicated." The words poured out of the computer, flooding over the admiral.

"If Dr. Beckett is trying to occupy two individuals at one time, I am forced to theorize that he will not be able to make a good job of it. The soul cannot be copied. Thus, to perform the tasks of this Leap, Dr. Beckett's soul would have to be torn in half. Opposite ends of his sum total will have to have been dragged apart from each other. Torn asunder."

Ziggy had gone silent then, as if the challenge of dealing in metaphysics had been too much for her. Al was embarrassed to discover his lower jaw hanging slack. While he closed it, mulling over what the computer had said, the machine spoke again.

"And if Dr. Beckett is working with only half a program, then he will be forced to draw upon the support programs already in place. He will have no choice. It is impossible to think otherwise. Thus I say again, ultimately the answer to your question will depend on the personalities of the twins."

The Control Room fell silent. Al had no response for

the computer. As the silently flashing lights continued to reflect off his face, the walls, each other, the admiral rolled over everything Ziggy had told him. Then the computer's voice came back, quietly adding, "Of course, I was not constructed to formulate opinions. I cannot be sure of the accuracy of the theory just presented."

"Okay, boys," Al said, closing down the memory of his last conversation with Ziggy, and picking up the discussion where they had left off. "What we need from you is some information, okay?"

"Look." Sam/Mark again. "I think that it's time you told us what this is all about. Are we dead? Are we in heaven? Are we back in the womb?" Sam's body sat forward, eagerness in his eyes.

Dr. Beeks was moving forward as well. Project policy was to not tell the Leapers where they were or what was going on. She had promised to not interfere unless she had to, but Al seemed to be headed for dangerous ground. Just before he reached the shoals she was afraid of, he veered off, saying, "All I can say is, that would be telling. You're here, and as soon as we can, we'll be sending you back home. But we can't do that unless we know a few things."

Al had also put Ziggy to the task of figuring out *why* Sam had Leaped. What was he supposed to be putting right. So far, the computer had not been able to discover anything major. With no input from Sam, they did not know what was happening "when" he was. And Ziggy needed that input to formulate possibilities. Thus, Al decided that until Tina and Gushie could find a way to get

173

the door opened so he could make it back to Sam, he would have to try to find out what this Leap was all about from the other end.

"So, now we're going to talk about your lives, boys. If you'd ever like to get back to them, you're going to have to let me know what was happening when you left. There is something wrong in those lives, gentlemen. Both of them. If it was only one of you, only that one would be here. So, there must be something coming to a head that involves both of you and until we figure out what it is—and this is not a threat, it's just a statement of fact—nobody's going anywhere."

Pulling up a chair, the admiral sat down next to the bed on which Sam's body was stretched. Rubbing his hands together, Al asked, "So, who wants to go first?"

CHAPTER
TWENTY-TWO

In a quirk of fate that Sam Beckett was unable to appreciate, he had managed to personify the old adage of the left hand not knowing what the right hand was doing.

In the minibus, he sat quietly behind the wheel. Neither he nor Klein talked much as they held back, trying to keep as much distance between themselves and the truck they had watched pull out of OR&T.

Ahead, in the rig in question, Sam was watching the road, not the cars behind him. He was more than a little nervous over the surprise addition of his two passengers and trying desperately not to show it.

"What's the matter, Ward?" asked the man sitting next to him. "What're you so damn jumpy about?"

"Me?" Asked Sam. "Jumpy? I'm not jumpy."

"The hell you're not," answered the large man. No longer content to merely shift his head to look at Ward, he turned his whole body in the cramped confines of the cab. Staring for a moment, he added, "You've been acting weird ever since you got into the cab."

"Yeah," added the second man, the one near the door. "Eddie's right. You've been creepin' me out, too. What're you so geared up about?"

"Guys" started Sam again, wondering just what was going on. "Guys. What do you want from me? I mean, Eddie, you bring this new dude along . . . I don't know who he is . . . you don't introduce us."

Talk like Ward, you idiot, Sam's mind raged at him. You're not Sam Beckett. You're Ward Ralston. *Talk like him!*

Immediately Sam pushed his back into the driver's seat, loosening his grip on the steering wheel. Forcing himself away from control of the situation, he let the part of him that felt most like Ward to flow forward.

"Hell," he said. "I ain't blind, you know. You're both packin' heat. I don't know this guy and I don't know what's goin' on and—believe it or not—I would actually like to know just what's comin' down."

Sam fished Ward's Marlboros out of his shirt pocket. Pulling a wooden match from the ashtray he struck it on a rough section of the dashboard. Firing the cigarette, he inhaled deeply while Eddie answered, "Okay, okay, keep your blood cool. Damn, you'd think we hadn't done this a thousand times. Ward Ralston, meet Skinner Valkin. Man, I bring the same spare three times in a row and all of a sudden you turn into nervous Nellie."

Sam extended his hand across Eddie's chest toward the other man. As they shook hands, he exhaled out the

176

window, shouting over the noise of the road.

"Please to meet ya, Skinner. You'll pardon me over wanting to have some idea who the new gunslinger is. You probably get curious every time some new guy comes into a room with a greased pit or a handful of steel."

"Don't sweat it," answered the man against the door in a semigood-natured voice. "I been known to sit with my back to the wall myself."

The three continued along the highway in silence, letting the radio fill the void. Sam was still curious as to why Eddie had started him out toward the desert. As far as he knew—all he knew—he should have been heading north toward Idaho. Instead they were moving east toward Nevada. After another hour and a half, he got his answer.

"Hey, shouldn't you be slowin' down?"

"What for?" asked Sam. His foot eased off the gas automatically. He had had his actions questioned on too many Leaps to not recognize the tone that told him he was not acting as expected.

As the rig began to slow, Eddie pointed out through the windshield toward the right and told him, " 'Cause that's our turnoff."

Sam shifted down, hitting his turn signal at the same time. Even having slowed their speed as soon as Eddie had cued him, he still made the turn with only seconds to spare. As he approached the end of the dark exit, he could see that the road branched not only to the left and the right, but also crossed over the intersecting road as well. Stopping at the posted sign, he turned slightly toward Eddie and asked, "Which way?"

Eddie looked at Sam for a long moment. Then suddenly, without warning, he pulled a .45 automatic out from beneath his jacket. Shoving it toward Sam's chest, he growled, "You go straight, and you pull over, and you stop this thing, and you do it now."

Sam started the rig rolling again. He did it slowly, making no sudden moves that might startle Eddie. Once they got across the road, he pulled up onto the shoulder at the first convenient spot. The second he turned off the engine, the gunman pushed against him, commanding, "Out."

Again Sam did as he was told without hesitation. He'd done something wrong, seriously wrong, and these guys didn't seem the type to forgive and forget. Even as he climbed out of the rig, his mind was racing to see how he might get through this night alive. Damn you, Wade, he thought. Didn't you do anything straight in your entire life?

As Sam's feet hit the ground, he saw that Eddie had moved out the same door, following him down. When he reached the roadway, he looked hard in every direction, making sure they were alone. It was an ink-dark stretch of road, one with no lights anywhere save a few far in the distance. With most of his attention focused on Sam, the rest on the cab above him, he shouted back up to Skinner, "Check the cab out."

"For what?" called back the other gunman.

"For anything. Just get the lights on and look the damn thing over." Then Eddie turned his full attention on Sam. Using his automatic as a pointer, he snarled,

178

"Get around the other side of the truck."

"Fine, sure. Whatever," he said, already walking. "But just tell me what's goin' on—will ya?"

As the two rounded the truck, Eddie pushed Sam up against the trailer roughly. The gunman's face was a mask of contradictions. Sam could see that he was confused—that he did not know what to make of Sam's lack of knowledge over what they were doing. Taking a step back, Eddie snarled, "Strip."

"What?" asked Sam, his mind trying to figure out what was happening. "Strip?"

"There's something too weird about you tonight, Ward. The only thing I can figure is that somebody got to you and now you're wearin' a wire."

"A wire?" asked Sam, confusion in his voice. He fumbled with the top button of his shirt for just a moment, then suddenly he realized what Eddie meant.

"Oh, hell," he said, relief filling his voice. "You think I've got a tape recorder in my jock strap." Sam starting undressing faster, laughing as he did so.

"What's so funny?"

"All of this. Jeez, me wear a wire. Oh, yeah." Sam got his shirt off and immediately dropped his hands to his belt. Unfastening it, he dropped his pants, pushing them down around his boots.

"There, see?" he asked, turning around slowly to make sure Eddie got a clear view in the dim light coming from the cab of his truck. "No hog factory CD players. Okay?"

Eddie stood his ground, not answering, simply staring at Sam. He did so for so long that Sam finally felt safe in pulling his pants back up and buckling them. As he grabbed his shirt up off the ground, he filled his face with a sheepish, almost shame-filled look. Then, taking a tentative step forward toward Eddie, he said, "I ain't playin' cops or nuthin' like that. I swear it. I can tell ya what the matter is. And maybe you'll like it, maybe ya won't. Not much I can do about it either way. But I'm tellin' ya, it got nothing to do with the cops."

"Okay, then," said Eddie, looking some small degree more comfortable. "Talk. What's goin' on?"

Sam took a deep breath and prayed that he could lie as well as Ward. "This ain't real easy for me, but I don't think gettin' shot and dumped in the desert would go too easy on me, either . . . so . . . well, all I can say is, you know I'm a man who likes his drink. Don't you?"

"Yeah. So what?"

"So, well . . . it's caught up to me."

"What're you talkin' about?"

"I'm sayin' that I've started gettin' blank patches in my memory. Stuff just don't hold like it used to. I remember you, and I know what we're doin' might be called—by some, mind you—as, well, wrong. I don't care. I don't give a shit what it is we're doin'. I just don't *remember* what it is."

Sam swallowed hard, not knowing what else he could say. Eddie stared at him, calculating. Buttoning his shirt halfway, Sam added, "Eddie, I got a wife and two good kids. If you don't want me to do whatever this is, I won't do it no more. I'll not even make this run. I'll take what I've got back and cancel my contract. I'll pay the penalties. Anything. But, man, don't kill me just for bein' a damn stupid drunk.''

The gunman considered the situation for a while longer, then said tentatively, ''I noticed you didn't offer me a drink tonight.''

''Because I stopped,'' said Sam, desperate to convince Eddie there was no need to kill him. ''I know I've been a hell-raiser all my life, and it ain't easy to turn my back on it. But I woke up the other morning and I felt as if my guts had been kicked out. I wasn't myself, I didn't know who I was. All I knew was I felt like I'd almost died during the night, and there was an empty JD bottle next to me. If it wasn't for my record book, I wouldn't of even known I was supposed to be here tonight.''

At that moment, Skinner stuck his head out the window and shouted down to the two men on the ground.

''Eddie—there ain't nothing I can see up here that don't look like it belongs.''

Sam looked across at the gunman. He had nothing left to offer. Whatever Eddie was going to do, he was going to have to do it on his own. Finally, the other man slid his .45 back under his coat, saying, ''Okay. So I believe you. That don't tell me what I do with you now.''

''What do you mean?''

''I mean now that you got yourself this convenient memory loss,'' he said in a sinister, suggestive tone, ''maybe you got yourself some religion along the way, too.''

''Don't be insultin','' laughed Sam, more from the release of tension that had come with Eddie reholstering his weapon. ''My book says this is a high-money job.

Where else am I gonna get green like this pays?''

"That's a good question," agreed Eddie. Motioning with his hand for Sam to start walking, the pair of them headed back for the driver's side of the rig. Within seconds they were back in the cab, Sam heading the rig down the back road Eddie pointed out. As they moved through the night, the gunman picked up his answer where he had left off, saying, "Listen, Ward, you still know what OR&T does—basically, I mean—right?''

"Yeah. They haul and store all the crap no one else wants to deal with.''

"Right, and they do pretty good by underbidding everyone else in sight.''

"And we . . ." said Sam, catching on to where Eddie was leading, "we help them keep those bids down. By being good back-to-nature types.''

"Back to nature?'' questioned Skinner.

"Yeah," said Sam with forced humor. "We take whatever damn waste garbage people want to get rid of, and we take it back to nature and dump it.''

Eddie laughed, his head nodding up and down. Skinner banged his left fist on the dashboard, his right against the outside door. Sam grinned himself. It wasn't a bad joke, considering the pressure he was under.

They hadn't traveled much farther when Eddie directed Sam to head for a private, fenced-off road. When they pulled up to the gate, Skinner jumped down and opened the lock, then clambered back up into the cab, leaving the gate open.

As they drove slowly down the rougher roadway, Sam's grin grew even wider. As far as he was concerned, things were back on track—things were going just fine. He had kept Ward from getting killed, and assured his big payoff. With the money he was getting from just this one job he knew he could parlay it into a bankroll ten times the size.

After all, he thought, when you know the future, it's not all that hard to make some halfway decent bets.

And what about the stuff you're dumping here tonight? Sam paused, thinking furiously. He could place a call—anonymous, of course—to the appropriate authorities. It was their job to clean up stuff like this, anyway, right? Hell, there might even be a reward in it for him, he played it right.

Seeing the smile spreading over Ward's face, Eddie asked, "So, you got no problems with any of this, right?"

"Well, sure. What's the big deal? I ain't no rocket scientist." Not hardly, thought Sam, rocket scientists aren't half as smart as I am. "But the crap we're haulin' ain't all that bad. It ain't gonna hurt nobody."

"No," answered Eddie with a small hesitation dragging through his voice. "But that isn't what you're being paid to dump, either."

In the far, dim distance, Sam saw a dilapidated old wooden barn. It was a large one, sided by two smaller structures. Skinner jumped down to the ground and opened up the fence surrounding the three buildings. Then he moved forward, pulling open the door to the barn. Through the doorway Sam could make out another trailer parked inside. It was bigger than his own, but nothing that his tractor could not handle.

"That's what you'll be dumping."

"What's in it?" asked Sam. "Somethin' worse than alkaline residue?"

"Oh, yeah," answered Eddie, laughing. "Hohoho-hoooho, yeah. A lot worse."

CHAPTER
TWENTY-THREE

Al had picked out his spiffiest suit. He knew Sam would be fairly vocal over how long it had taken the admiral to reach him. The suit would make a nice distraction.

He looked himself over in the mirror, making sure every detail was perfect. Every fold in his tailored silk blazer was sharp. He remembered when he bought it that the salesman had told him that it was a very stylish shade of "eggplant."

Instantly he had flashed to a childhood memory. One of the other Italian kids in the orphanage, Lenny Cecolini, had always talked about how his grandmother had fried eggplant for Sunday dinner every week. Lenny could make the meal come alive for them—talking about the breading, the seasoning, the smell of the tomatoes as they boiled down into paste. Al and the rest of the Italian kids had drooled, even though most of them had never even tasted eggplant before.

It had been a long time before the admiral had realized what it was in Lenny's tales of his grandmother's kitchen that they had all really been hungry for.

"That was a long time ago," he told his image in the mirror. He straightened out a crease in the dark silk of his sleeve. As the fold smoothed away, he stared into the deep rich color of his mirror-image's jacket, and then whispered again, "A very, *very* long time ago."

Turning on his heel abruptly, he left the mirror, shutting the door behind him. Once out in the hall he headed straight for the Control Room. The word was that Ziggy would soon be ready. Al intended to be ready when the computer was.

With both Verbeena's and Ziggy's help, the admiral had pieced together a rough idea of what was happening to Sam back in 1986. Ward had admitted to dumping illegal toxics in the desert and the mountains for a company named Oregon Removal & Transport. That fact had caught Mark's attention. The other Ralston let Al know that he was part of an environmental group tracking the corporation's movements. The two brothers had exchanged rather heated words over their respective points of view, "tree-hugger" being the kindest.

Armed with this information, Al had left Verbeena to moderate the escalating verbal battle and put Ziggy to the task of following the Ralston brothers' lives, as well as the court history of OR&T—concentrating on '86 and beyond. The computer had buckled down to the task.

With luck, Al thought as he marched down the hall, that damn rust bucket will have at least some small idea as to what kind of situation Sam is in before I can even get back there.

As the admiral had turned the corner onto the last hall leading to the Control Room, his pace slowed. He had tried twice this Leap to reach Sam and had been denied.

"Third time's the charm," he told himself softly as his fingers gripped the door handle. As he began to push it inward, a small voice in the back of his head whispered, "Three strikes and you're out."

"Thanks for the reminder," he said under his breath, then pushed the door open and walked in on the work crew.

"So," he demanded, dismissing the fear from his voice, "is the damn bucket of bolts working now or isn't she?"

My God, thought Al suddenly, how many times have I said that this week?

From the look in Gushie's eyes, he decided that whatever the number was, it was one time too many. Knowing everyone else was feeling the same kind of strain he was, Al decided to ease up, and maybe break the tension. To do so, he simply repeated his thought out loud.

"I was just asking myself, how many times have I said that sentence this week?"

"Thirteen," answered Ziggy.

"Thirteen?" asked Tina. "That's all?"

While Al scowled at the redhead, the computer responded, telling the engineer, "The admiral has said 'Is that damn bucket of bolts working now or isn't she?' only thirteen times. You may be confusing that sentence with 'Is that damn hunk of tin ready to go or not?' That

187

one he has said only three times."

Gushie used a hand to cover his mouth. Tina started to smile. While they tried to keep from laughing, Ziggy continued, the female tones of the computer's voice growing a shade colder with every few words.

" 'Can't you get this piece of junk going?' Twice. 'Is her Metal Majesty working or not?' Once."

The word "once" was so drenched in venom that Gushie and Tina could no longer control themselves. The engineer and the programmer broke out laughing. As Ziggy continued to talk, their laughter grew in volume.

" 'Fix it.' Eighteen times."

Al interrupted, pasting a shocked look on his face.

"Eighteen? Really?"

"Yes, Admiral," answered the computer, a haughty tone in her voice. "Eighteen times. This week."

"My, my," added Al, doing his best to look abashed. He made a "tsk tsk" sound, then turned on Gushie, fixing the programmer with a harsh stare as he asked, "So, tell me, laughing boy . . . after eighteen tries . . . is that damn hunk of tin ready to go or not?" As everyone got suddenly quiet, Al pulled a cigar from his pocket. "That's fourteen. Do I hear fifteen?"

"No, sir," answered Gushie, mopping at his forehead. Bending down to pick up the cloth tool spread he had laid out on the floor near his last work site, he said, "I think the hun . . . I think Ziggy is back in one piece."

"And can that one piece finally do the job?"

"Yes, sir . . . I think the situation has changed to where we've got a clear shot back."

188

"What's changed?" asked the admiral. If there was new information, as they used to say in the Navy, the C.O.'s supposed to know.

Gushie, chastised, said, "Ziggy . . . you want to do the fill-in?"

"Admiral," the computer's voice purred, "the two points which both represented Dr. Beckett's whereabouts in the time line were too far apart for clear transmission earlier. Since the beam signal attuned to your body is linked to Dr. Beckett's presence, it was impossible to send you back before because the receiver in 1986—Dr. Beckett—could not pick up your signal. Now, two things have happened."

Al folded his arms over his chest, restraining his urge to groan. Ziggy simply could not be hurried along. To try was only to invite time-wasting arguments.

"First, Tina was able to boost my ability to open the door over a wide range. It is a temporary boost, one that will require enormous power increases, and one that will also only be available for short intervals. You will only be able to stay with Dr. Beckett for short periods of time. Hopefully they will suffice. Before, the relay focus was as wide as the width of Dr. Beckett's arms. Now, however, it is as wide as the distance between the two Ralston brothers."

"Tina," asked the admiral, "you boosted Ziggy's power to go across states?"

"No, Admiral," interrupted the computer. "That is the second thing which has happened. The two Dr. Becketts have come into a much closer proximity to each other."

Al gritted his teeth, wishing Ziggy would just hurry up and get to the point. He was desperate to get back to Sam, before too much more time passed—before it was too late. Regardless of his worries, however, he settled in to hear what the computer had to say. As much as he hated to admit it, he needed all the information Ziggy could supply before he went through the door.

"Given the data you relayed to me earlier, Admiral, I believe . . . estimating from what we have to go on, considering Dr. Beckett's time into the Leap, and the Ralston brothers' recollections of what they were to be doing this week, and adding in, of course, both of Dr. Beckett's present locations . . . it is safe to assume that if we—"

"Get to the point, damnit!" Al shouted. "Sam could be dying back there. Anything could be happening this time. Save the double-talk and stop covering your ass and just *give*!"

Good going, idiot, he told himself. Now you've done it . . . Now you've really done it.

Without missing a beat, Ziggy continued on unperturbed. The computer's artificial feminine tones poured out easily over the tension Al had created with only the barest hint of hidden smugness.

"We send your door image back on a wide focus with Tina's added boost of power that we should be able to connect you to one or the other of Dr. Beckett's current hosts."

"Wonderful," said Al with more than a hint of impatience lurking in his voice. "When do we get to try it?"

"Anytime you wish," responded Ziggy. "After we have finished your routine briefing."

"There's more?" asked the admiral.

"Much more," the computer assured him. "I will attempt to be brief, and only cover the basics you would be able to understand."

God, how I hate this machine sometimes, thought Al.

And Sam, he added, sometimes I hate you for building it. You couldn't watch something normal like *Star Trek* like the rest of the kids and end up inventing something useful like faster-than-light travel—no, you had to watch *Time Tunnel* and end up giving us this Project Quantum Leap.

"Our best probability is that Ward Ralston is making one of his illegal dumps right now. Dr. Beckett's present location corresponds with the information you obtained from him previously, Admiral. Since Mark Ralston's position is within a half mile of his brother, it is assumed that, given his observance of OR&T's illicit doings, he is at present spying on his brother's activities."

"Fine," said Al, taking his position, priming his handlink, "great. Good job. Now . . . I'm all routinely briefed." Sticking the handlink under his arm, he slapped his palms together, saying, "So, let's go. Let's move."

"I would like to give you one last bit of information, Admiral."

"What? What now?"

"It is information that, I am afraid, due to your own regulations, can only be imparted to you. If you would step into the Imaging Chamber?"

191

Al hesitated for a second, wondering what had happened. The only kind of information Ziggy was restricted from sharing with anyone but him were facts pertaining to shifts in time—changes in the time stream from the facts the computer alone knew to be the way things had been before Sam Beckett had stepped into the Accelerator.

Al looked at Gushie and Tina with an expression of pained helplessness. They were obviously puzzled.

"All right, Zig." He walked up the ramp, into the Imaging Chamber. The door shut behind him.

"Spill it, Ziggy—what's changing?"

"The area of the Mojave Desert in which Ward Ralston attempted to make his last illegal dumping has a major fault area running through it. If he had made his dump there, the consequences would have been serious."

"What exactly does 'serious' mean here?"

"Oregon Removal & Transport was an ingenious company in a criminal sense," answered Ziggy. "They would mix the shipments their haulers were making. Client A would dump client C's waste, client C would handle client B's waste, et cetera. Whenever they would be raided, they would never have the merchandise they were supposed to have. Ward Ralston was one of their key players . . . moving much of their most toxic waste. Right now, Dr. Beckett, if he is following the patterns of Ward Ralston's life, is about to dump approximately nine and a half tons of dangerously antiquated chemical weapons in a mine shaft in the Mojave—one directly over the fault lines."

"Hazards?" asked Al, using the last military term he had for such weapons. "What levels?"

"They were all G-series, fast-acting gas and vapor agents. Thousands of pounds each of nerve, blister, blood, and choking agents."

"Why do you keep harping on that fault line," asked the admiral, afraid he already knew the answer.

"Because in 1991 a minor quake ran through the series of strata in that area. Only registering 2.874 on the Richter scale, it was ignored by the public at large. If Ward Ralston had left his decaying cargo there, it would have been another matter entirely, however."

"How bad would it have been?"

"My best estimates, incorporating likely probability after factoring the winds recorded at the time, and the fact that the mine itself would have acted like a pumping box, indicate that the chemicals would have been spread over hundreds of thousands of square miles. Fatalities would have topped three hundred thousand. Near casualties, those merely hospitalized, left blind, bleeding internally, speechless, et cetera, would almost assuredly be capped at one and three-quarters millions."

"But, Zig," asked Al, fear creeping into the sides of his voice, "why is this important? After all, you said that Ward never got away with this."

"True. On this night, both of the Ralstons were murdered in the desert by two men in OR&T's employ. The dump was never made. OR&T was shut down in 1987 through evidence obtained from a witness, a Dr. Franklin Klein."

"Ziggy, what are you saying?"

Al tried to catch his breath, tried to continue talking, but could not find the words. Sucking down a deep breath, the admiral reached inside himself for the last of his remaining resolve, then asked in a quiet voice, "What are you telling me? That Sam is going to die tonight, or that he's going to keep these guys from dying, and let these chemicals get dumped?"

"My figures show an 85.15 percent chance of the latter shift. In this new timeline, Ward Ralston is not dead. Mark Ralston, however, is dead. Oregon Removal & Transport is still in business. And in 1991, on the fifth of June, at 9:27, the quake that previously went unnoticed by the world hit the dump site, injuring and or killing over two million people over a period of three days."

"85 percent chance," muttered Al, standing in the center of the Control Room, stunned. He moved his handlink up to where he could read it, to where he could see the figures Ziggy was quoting. Before he could focus on its miniature screen, however, the computer corrected his whisper, saying, "92.38 percent."

"You said . . ."

"Time waits for no man, Admiral," said the computer, its voice sounding colder than ever to him. "I would have thought you knew that by now."

Al let his hand slowly drop back to his side. Ziggy triggered the link created by the shared neural network on the computer's biochips without having to be told.

As the familiar hum started, the admiral knew it would take less than a second for him to suddenly begin sharing Sam's perceptions of his surroundings. As far as all his senses would be able to tell, he would disappear from the Project. In actuality, only a projection of Al would be catapulted back to the Mojave Desert—his body would stay right where it was.

The admiral thought about that fact. He had never liked being with Sam in spirit only. Being able only to advise him, feed him statistics and facts from Ziggy. But as he stepped through the crackling rectangle of white energy that led to the past, he thought about the load of old, unstable weapons about to be manhandled like so many bags of garbage.

Although he was loath to admit it, for once he was not as hostile to the idea of leaving his body behind.

CHAPTER
TWENTY-FOUR

Sam had already moved his tractor out from under his trailer. He had unhitched it on a practically level-perfect stretch of desert, a spot so smooth he figured that had to be one of the major reasons it had been picked in the first place.

The land belonged to Oregon Removal & Transport under another name. They had bought the acreage and left it as it was at the time of purchase to keep from arousing any suspicions from their neighbors. The old barn had served the corporation in good stead for a number of years in rotation with other places just like it.

Taking down the jumbo flashlight Ward kept in his cab, he had gotten underneath and checked its support legs and sand shoes, making sure it would stand firm even in the high desert winds until he could return for it.

By now Sam had pieced together the overall workings

of Oregon Removal & Transport's surprisingly simple scheme. The people who were supposed to be moving the harsh loads never had them. The trailers were always switched a few miles outside of town. No matter where someone might be looking for something, it was always on a different truck, in some other state, going in the opposite direction.

Loads like he had in his own trailer were no problem to dispose of properly. It just took time and money. And saving time and money was apparently the name of OR&T's game. Proper containment of anything, even nuclear waste, was possible—it was merely expensive. But if one just went out and dumped it somewhere, then suddenly hundreds of thousands of dollars could be saved.

All one had to be was ruthless, reckless, and a bit of a gambler.

Or an idiot, thought Sam. Ward Ralston, you're just about the biggest fool I ever Leaped into. With a plan this stupid, I'm surprised these morons are still in business.

He wondered about who was in charge at OR&T. He wondered at how long they thought they could continue to get away with such a sloppy scheme. It was far too dependent on payoffs and intimidation. Sooner or later one little slip was going to bring the whole house of cards down—the way it did all grand criminal schemes.

Man, thought Sam, walking back toward his tractor, if I had the controlling shares in this company, this would be about the time I'd be selling out to my partners and heading for the nearest nonextradition border. Between the environmentalists and the Superfund and all the rest, the coming years are not the time to be involved in this kind of scam.

"No, sir," he whispered to the night air. "This is going to be the last of this life for ol' Ward Ralston. Clean livin' from here on in. Your idiot days are over, Ward m'boy."

"What'd you say, Ward?"

"Nuthin', Eddie," Sam shouted back, not realizing the gunman had come down from the cab. "Just talkin' to myself. Bad truck driver habit—you know."

"Yeah, yeah," answered Eddie in a distracted voice.

Sam could see Skinner's feet moving on the other side of the tractor. He could also see that Eddie had his gun in hand. Coming up alongside the gunman, he asked in a low voice, "What's doin'? We got company?"

"Nothing, probably."

"Nothing?"

"Naw," answered Eddie, seeming to relax. "Skinner thought he heard something. I don't know, he just got jumpy, I guess . . . then he got me jumpy."

"So, it's catchin'. You sure there's nothin' goin' on? I just been gettin' my life back together. I don't fancy spendin' what I got in no rock wall motel."

"Don't sweat it, Ward," replied Eddie. As the gunman stared off into the night sky, still scanning the horizon, he added, "Listen, if I have to go back to the joint, they ain't going to be quoting me the day rate. They'll be asking for first and last month's rent, and the security. Believe me, if there's anyone who don't want to see the inside of the can again, it's me."

"Still . . ." said Sam, suddenly deeply uneasy. "Maybe we should look around a little."

"Yeah," agreed Eddie. "Maybe we should. But not you. You get that other trailer hitched up and ready to go. Skinner and me'll give everything a last once-over."

Sam agreed to the plan, moving off toward his tractor once more. Putting his foot up on the fuel tank step, he grabbed hold of the assist handle and hoisted himself up to the driver's side door. He pulled it open just as a flash of white light appeared in the cab, startling him so badly he almost lost his grip, and gasped loudly.

"Hi, Sam," said Al, sitting on the passenger side of the cab. "Miss me?"

"What was that?" shouted Skinner.

Hurriedly Sam shouted down to the gunmen, "I just slipped. Almost fell on my ass. Didn't mean to scare ya."

Skinner muttered something Sam could not make out. Quickly pulling himself into the cab, Sam slammed the door and then turned to Al.

"What the hell do you want?"

"Hey," the Observer answered, sounding somewhat hurt, "don't go and get sloppy on me."

"I'll tell you what," answered Sam under his breath, "why don't you just skedaddle back to the Project and forget all about me."

"Sam, I don't think this is the time for jokes."

"I'm not making one," answered Sam. Digging his keys out of his pocket, he rammed them into the ignition, telling Al, "So why don't you get out of here and leave me alone?"

"Leave you alone?" The admiral hovered in the cab. "Hey, this is not the time to be throwing a hissy fit over the fact that it took me a while to get here . . ."

"I don't care that you're late. I was hoping that I'd never see you again."

"Sam . . . ?"

Sam took a quick look in both his side-view mirrors to check the positions of the two gunmen. He saw them both in the distance, moving farther away from the tractor. Satisfied that they would not be able to hear him, he turned to Al. Keeping his voice low anyway, he said, "I'm not going on, Al. I'm staying here."

"What are you talking about? Are you gone nutty all of a sudden? You can't stay here."

"I can try. Look, I Leap to make right what went wrong, yeah? Well, Ward Ralston's what's wrong. And my being here makes it right. So go back to the Project and tell them I'm fine, and they should just go get lives of their own."

"Sam, you've got to be kidding me."

"Get yourself a new knight in shining armor, Al. I'm finished with this gig. Do you understand? It's my turn now. Now Sam Beckett gets a life. Now I get kids and a wife and some time to watch the daisies grow. Do you read me?"

Al stared in almost complete disbelief. He watched as Sam turned away from him, switching on the tractor, getting it into gear, moving it toward the barn across the flat, dry desert plane. Throughout the long moment, he did not know what to say.

His Sam Beckett was the most giving, caring man he

had ever met. To hear him talk about stealing another man's life as if it were his given due ... he simply did not know how to respond. Then his eye was caught by figures changing on his handlink. Suddenly the future Ziggy had explained back in the Imaging Chamber was a 98.3 percent certainty.

Somehow, the admiral found his voice.

"You're out of your mind. Do you get me? Tell me, do you have any idea what's in that trailer you're headed for?"

"Something bad."

"Something bad?" Al slapped his forehead. "That's all you know? Something bad?"

"Yeah, Al, it's something bad. Something bad that I intend to dump wherever I'm told to so I can get a big bag of cash and get on with my new life. So don't start any lectures, because it doesn't matter anymore."

"Doesn't matter? *It doesn't matter?!*"

Sam threw the tractor into reverse, swinging it around and heading it back toward the barn. He moved it carefully, waiting for the feel of the frame rail to slide under the body of the trailer, waiting for the feel of the kingpin sliding into the trailer connection. Satisfied that he had everything in position, he snarled, "No, Al, it doesn't matter."

As Sam shut down the tractor, the admiral screamed at him, "That thing's crammed up with G-series chemical slop. Nerve gas, blood agents, chokers, vomiters— it's the wonderful world of toxic agents back there, pal, and you're their goddamned Walt Disney!"

Sam leaped down to the ground, leaving the Observer

behind him. As he headed into the barn to ready the new trailer for moving, he shouted, "Leave me alone, Al. Go away. Go collect your retirement and chase women and smoke cigars. Go back to drinking. Go do whatever you want. Just leave me out of your plans from now on."

Al moved through the back of the cab and down onto the floor of the barn. While Sam busied himself with the rig's gladhands and electrical connections, the admiral continued to berate him.

"The stuff you're going to dump, do you know where you're putting it? You're dropping it on top of a fault line. Ziggy says in 1991 a quake is going to rip it up and spread it around. It turns out to be one of those bad breaks for southern California, unseasonably high winds *and* a dust cloud of killer chemicals. Do you want to know what happens, Sam?"

"No," he growled. "Not really."

"Well, you're going to. Over two million people, Sam. Two million of them. Dead and dying. Crippled for life. It's a mess so bad you don't know which ones to call the lucky ones—the ones that make it or the ones that don't."

"It doesn't matter, Al. Everybody dies. Everybody. Everybody except me. I just keep bouncing around from life to life, cleaning up the messes every useless boob who can't think for himself has made out of what they've got. Well, now I get something. Let the great unknown Leap someone into me and fix my life for a change."

"Sam," pleaded Al, confused and desperate, "you can't do this. You're going to change history—the way

Hitler did. And for just about the same reasons.''

Before Sam could answer, Eddie's voice came from somewhere out in the dark.

"Ward? Where are you?"

"In the barn. I'm just sealin' off the light wires and all.''

"Come on out here, would you?"

"Sure," he said. Aiming his flashlight down toward the dry dirt floor of the barn, Sam headed back for the outside.

As he went, he pointed forward and whispered, "That's where I'm going, Al. You and the Project, you're back in—in my past. That's 1986 out there—that's my future.''

He stepped outside the barn's doors and found Eddie and Skinner approaching in the distance. They were not alone, however. In the moonlight Sam could see that they were half dragging, half pushing along a man who looked very familiar—even in the dark. Very familiar. A man whose face looked like the one he had been seeing in the mirror for the last week. Exactly like it.

CHAPTER
TWENTY-FIVE

"Who—who is that?" asked Sam, standing frozen in the barn doorway.

"Oh, right—him," said Al, "I guess I didn't have time to mention. That's your twin brother, Mark, the college professor. You haven't talked to each other in about fifteen years. Something about being loyal to the person who raised you." The admiral's words came in a low tone, one that was both bitter and hostile.

Moving closer to the Sam in the barn, he said, "But I wouldn't get too concerned about family reunions right now. Ziggy says that your new buddies over there"—he pointed toward Eddie and Skinner with a dismissive, contemptuous wave—"they're going to kill him."

Eddie moved forward, a dusty video camera in one hand, his .45 in the other. Next to him came Skinner, dragging Mark Ralston forward. In a voice without a trace of humor, Eddie asked Ward Ralston, "Who the hell is this, you ask? That's what we'd like to know. Who is this guy? And don't say something stupid like he's your twin brother.''

Sam looked over at himself, the himself he had gotten to know over the past week. Outside of the rapidly puffing eye and the blood pouring from his nose, it was the same face, topped by the same straight black hair, on the same head, atop the same body. Trying to contain his shock, he stammered, ''It—it—it, I mean, it may sound stupid, but well, yes, look at him. He *is* my twin brother.''

Eddie stared, without a clue as to where he should go next. Skinner merely waited patiently. No one had ever paid him to do any thinking in his entire life. With one hand around Mark Ralston's left wrist, the other holding his silver .38 snubnose to the man's head, his job was to contain the one Ralston while his partner figured out what he should do with the other.

Moving across the barn, Al went to the Sam under the gun, asking him, ''I know you can't talk, but you can nod. You in there, Sam?'' When Mark's head went up and down, the admiral went on, letting him know that he was also across the way in Mark's brother, and that that version of him was giving up on Leaping.

When Sam merely stared out of Mark's eyes in confusion, Al continued, telling him, ''Oh, yeah, says Leaping's for suckers. Says he's fed up and he's not going back.''

Looking at himself across the way, Sam/Mark yelled, ''You can't do that! *We* can't do that!''

''Sez who?'' demanded Sam/Ward in the barn. ''This

205

is America . . . brother. I can do whatever I want. Free, white, twenty-one, all that good stuff—remember?''

"Shut up, both of you," demanded Eddie. He waved his weapon back and forth from one's chest to the other's.

Sam/Ward stopped moving, putting his hands up in a halting motion, saying, "Hey, careful with that thing!"

"Why, Ward?" asked the gunman, taking a threatening step forward. "Why should I?"

"Because I'm on your side, remember? We're in this together. What he's doin' here, I got no idea." Turning toward the other Ralston, he said, "What *are* you doin' here, Mark? This ain't exactly the time for a family reunion."

"I was looking for proof that OR&T was dumping illegally in the desert. I was going to film it and turn it over to the authorities."

"Do you hear him, Sam?" shouted Al. "Does that kind of talk sound familiar? There was a time that was the only kind of talk I heard out of *your* mouth."

Al stared from the one Sam to the other, not knowing what to do. He saw the Ralston twins, of course, the same way Eddie and Skinner and anyone else in 1986 would have seen them. But because of the process that combined his brain tissues with computer chips, he also saw Sam Beckett. Six feet tall, green eyes, and brown hair with a single streak of white at his left temple. Familiar. Reassuring. This time, however, he saw something else.

As he stared at the Sam in the barn—actually looked into his face—he saw something he had never seen be-

206

fore. This Sam's eyes were narrowed, suspicious, greedy. His lips were pressed against each other, the muscles of his mouth pulling them tight against his teeth. He looked like a weasel, his face twitching, eyes darting left and right.

Al stalked back to peer at the other Sam. He was also somehow different. That familiar face was blank, practically innocent. Dr. Sam Beckett was a man who disliked a lot of the world—but he at least understood it. This Sam Beckett was guileless, helpless, looking to Al as if he considered self-interest a dirty word. The Sam he knew would have thought of at least a bad lie rather than telling two killers with guns that he had come to film them so he would have the evidence he needed to send them to jail.

Looking at the two men, Al remembered his previous conversation with Ziggy, the one where she had explained to him the possible side-effects Sam might experience from Leaping into twins.

Oh, my God, thought Al. The Zig was right.

Shouting to both the Sams at the same time, Al told them, "You idiots—both of you. Listen to me. You've been cut in half. Ziggy said it was possible. Your upper brain functions have been separated from the primal ones. Survival versus altruism."

Both Sams stared at the point where Al was standing. Eddie and Skinner looked at the pair of them, seemingly staring into empty space.

"The two of you, one of you thinking only of himself, the other one thinking of everyone else—both of you saying damn the consequences—it's like watching a balanced Senate funding committee vote appropriations.''

"What are you two looking at?''

Sam/Ward turned to Eddie, his mind racing. If Al was right, he could not let anything happen to Mark Ralston. There was no telling what might happen if the two gunmen fulfilled Ziggy's prophesy. He might die. They both might die. Or worse yet, he might be reunited with the conscience from which he had finally been freed, and forced to go on Leaping.

"Eddie . . . listen. Twins, they do goofy things. One gets hurt, the other feels it. You can't help it. But look, don't worry about that. I can straighten this thing out. Let me talk to him for a minute.''

When the gunman did not move, Sam/Ward said, "He's a college professor. He's not doin' this alone. Someone's sure to know he's out here. That makes him tougher to kill. But bein' a college professor might also mean he's smart enough to listen to reason. Besides, if he won't . . .'' Sam shrugged, indicating that he didn't care one way or the other. "You can always kill him later.''

Al's blood went cold. He listened to the tone in Sam's voice, practically unable to believe his friend had been able to produce it. It was totally devoid of pity, and not the product of a performance. It was a voice straight from the reptilian cortex of the brain—brutal and hard, and ultimately convincing.

Eddie stepped aside, saying, "Sure—what the hell. See what he's got to say.''

Sam/Ward walked the rest of the way over to his "brother.'' While Skinner maintained his grip on Sam/

Mark, his other self said, "All right, now listen to me. Not to anything else—just to me."

Sam pointed to himself as he talked, specifically to his eyes. Hoping the half of him off in Mark's body understood where he was going, he said, "You wanted to bag OR&T. Be a big shot to your college buddies, be on the eleven o'clock news, score some points with the Sierra Club, whatever. But now tell me, serious—did you know I was here? I mean, you were lookin' to stick the bad guys in jail. All right, fine, hip hip hooray . . . but did you know that meant sending me to jail, too?"

Catching on to his role in the charade Sam/Ward had started, Sam/Mark answered, "No. I had no idea you were a part of this."

"That's what I thought. Now look, Mark . . ."

Sam/Ward continued on, making an impassioned speech that ran from brothers looking out for each other to what his sister-in-law, niece, and nephew would do with their uncle dead and father in jail. Meanwhile, Sam/Mark ran scenarios through his head, finally coming up with the one he thought his "twin" was working with.

Sam/Ward walked away from his "brother," continuing to talk animatedly, using the jumbo flashlight in his hand as a baton. He gave Sam/Mark several opportunities to make complacent noises, ones that told Eddie and Skinner he knew how to cooperate.

"So, now why don't you just tell Eddie and Skinner here that they don't need to kill you."

As the two gunmen unconsciously shifted their positions so as to be able to better hear Sam/Mark's answer,

Sam/Ward gave his twin a look that said *now's the moment.*

Instantly Sam/Ward brought the heavy flashlight he was holding down on Eddie's hand. The gunman's .45 dropped, bouncing off into the darkness. The other Sam had acted at the same instant, shifting his weight to throw the unprepared Skinner off balance.

"Yeah, yeah," shouted Al, pumping his fists in tight, hard jabs, "that's it. That's it! Get 'em, boys!"

Sam/Ward followed his strike against Eddie with a swinging full body kick that planted his boot against the side of the gunman's head. It was a rocking blow, one that sent Eddie staggering. A second kick, a high, straight scissor-thrust, caught the gunman squarely in the chest, propelling him against the grill of Ward's truck with force. His head slammed into it hard, bending the metal.

Outside the barn, Sam/Mark wrestled with Skinner over the .38. When his "brother" had given the signal, Sam/Mark shifted his weight and hooked his foot behind Skinner's leg. A jerk had sent the gunman staggering, unable to hold on to Sam/Mark without losing his balance. His gun hand had floundered wildly, trying to keep him on his feet, giving Sam/Mark a chance to grab it. Spinning Skinner by the wrist, Sam/Mark stepped into the gunman's approaching body and then ducked under it, flipping him up and over.

Skinner hit the ground hard enough to send a cloud of sand flying out from under him. Before he could recover his breath, Sam/Mark was on top of him, smashing him across the throat, cutting off his air. Skinner dropped his weapon, the .38 all but forgotten as he grabbed at his throat, hacking for air.

Taking the gunman's flopping hair in his hands, Sam/Mark pulled the man's face up and punched him once solidly. Sam/Mark stood up, leaving Skinner unconscious on the ground. Turning, he watched his other self slam Eddie in the side of the head once more.

"Yeah, oh, *yeah!*" shouted Al. The admiral was practically dancing as he bellowed, "Now *that's* the way it's done."

Sam looked over at Sam. The truck driver was breathing harder than the professor. Too many cigarettes and empty liquor bottles.

As the pair straightened up, catching their breath, dusting themselves off, Al said, "This is great. This is just great. This is the way things are supposed to be. Now, let's get these goons roped up and turned in and get this Leap over with."

"You two go ahead and do what you want," said Sam/Ward. Heading back toward his tractor, he said, "Me? Like I told you before—I'm out of here."

"Sam," said Al, looking from one Beckett to the other, "what are you talking about?"

"Just what I said." Picking up his flashlight, Sam/Ward said, "Do what you want. Just leave me out of it."

He clicked his flashlight on and then off, on and then off, making sure it still worked. Then he turned to Al and himself, telling them, "I ain't Leaping anymore."

CHAPTER
TWENTY-SIX

"Come again?" asked Sam/Mark. "I'm afraid I didn't catch that last thing you said."

"No," answered Sam/Ward. Dropping all pretense of Ward from his voice, he turned away from his other self, saying, "You caught it. You're choosing not to, though, for your own purposes. Just like me."

Tossing his flashlight up through the window of his cab, Sam/Ward turned back on himself, saying, "I choose not to Leap anymore. All right? You do it." Walking back toward his other self, his fingers tensing and untensing, he shouted, "You want to set the universe right, make it run along the right cosmic tracks—you do it."

Getting up face-to-face with his "brother," Sam/Ward pointed over to Al.

"You two go on without me. Go on, Leap out of here into the next poor sucker's life. I'd rather take my chances here with these two and whatever kind of a sap your half of this Leap turns out to be than go on with this farce we keep playing out."

"It's not like we have any choice in this," said Sam/Mark, putting his hand up to catch Sam/Ward's wrist. Yanking at him, trying to force him to listen, he said, "We wrecked time. Both of us. You may remember that. It was *both* of us that built the Project—both of us who stepped into the Accelerator. We both took it upon ourselves to make the next giant leap for mankind. Now it's up to both of us to fix it."

"No way," shouted Sam/Ward back at himself. Shaking off his other self's hand, he turned back to his rig, inspecting the connections he had been working on earlier. Leaning against the trailer he could see that the kingpin had not set entirely, which pleased him.

All the easier to dump this mess, he thought, and just up and get the hell out of here.

Turning away from the trailer, he moved back toward the cab, yelling again, "No way. Not anymore. Sure, I was all for traveling in time. Why not? Another feather in our cap, another shot at another Nobel. We had nothing else in our life, no wife, no children, so why not."

Al stepped forward, his shoulders hunched, palms held out. It tore him apart watching his friend arguing with himself, cursing himself. One part of his mind could not even comprehend what he was seeing. Another part understood all too well. He moved forward toward the pair, keeping his tone calm and reasonable.

"Fellas, let's calm down here. Okay?"

"Stay out of this, Al," said one of the Sams—the

admiral not actually sure which one.

"And while we're on the subject, I can tell you *why* women never get serious about us," added the Sam in Ward Ralston's body. "That's another one I can lay at your feet."

"Oh, so Donna was my fault—huh?"

"You're damn right she was," answered Sam/Ward. Like Sam/Mark, he could not remember why they had not stayed with Donna Elesee. She was just a memory that haunted them at rare moments, plaguing them. But knowing that it had to bother his other self as much as it did him, he went on brutally, saying, "You're the one that always had to keep pressing on, always had to get one more degree, one more doctorate, make one more discovery. You were the one that didn't want to have a family—didn't know how to make time for anyone else—didn't care about anything except finding out how much more you could cram inside our head."

Al froze, not knowing what to say. How could he tell Sam that in some timelines he had never lost Donna? That she was his wife, still waiting back at the Project for him as she had since the day he first Leaped? Like his relationship with Tina, Sam's with Donna was constantly changing. When he'd finally been able to get back to Sam this time, she was not back at the Project. When he returned, she very well might be.

To see his friend in such misery—literally one step away from tearing himself apart—the sight hurt Al like nothing he could remember. He wanted to comfort both of them at the same time he wanted to slap them both for acting like spoiled children. Before he could act on

214

any impulse, however, the mood of the fight shifted, away from the things the Sams could not remember, focusing on things which they could.

"And what would you have done?" Sam/Mark shouted back at himself, refusing to listen to his primal side, pushing away its vulgar desires as he had his entire life. "Where would you have taken us? To parties so we could have killed off our brain cells with drugs and liquor? I know you wanted to—I had to fight you every time there was an opportunity."

"Damn right I wanted to," Sam/Ward threw back at himself. "You are so right I wanted to. Kill a few brain cells? Sure. Why not? Maybe we wouldn't have ended up in this mess we're in now if we weren't so endlessly smart."

"No, of course not. Why bother thinking? Why put our brains to any use? That would be the responsible thing to do. But responsibility, that's not your thing, apparently. You'd rather we went into the Army so we could shoot off guns and drop bombs on people—so we could end up with our name etched in black stone—like Tom."

Sam/Ward's palm shot forward at lightning speed, slamming against Sam/Mark's chest. Sam/Mark's hand came up at the same time, moving at the same speed, striking its target with equal force.

"Liar!" they bellowed at each other, both suddenly remembering what the one had forgotten. "Tom didn't die. I saved him! I fixed that!"

The Sams staggered from the pair of violent blows, then each charged the other. They grabbed mindlessly for any hold they could manage. There was no style to their fighting, no attempt to think out a pattern of attack. Neither one of them seemed able to pull back, to wait for a proper moment to turn their foe's weight or rage against them. Pushing and shoving, they broke apart, and then engaged again, punching each other wildly. Al watched the two shapes struggling in the ebony pitch of the barn, not knowing what to do, what outcome to pray for.

As he stood by helplessly, a well-placed thrust from one Sam shot past the other's shifting head. Another fist came up, wilder, more erratic—its very unpredictability helping it connect. The thrower of the punch leaped forward, getting his arms around his target. The force of his attack staggered the pair. Both men fell over, crashing against the sand roughly, rolling away in the darkness.

"Sam, Sam," shouted Al, "for God's sake, are you crazy . . . both of you? There're guys with guns over here who might wake up. Sam, get a hold of yourself—yourselves!"

But there was nothing the admiral could do to get their attention. They were consumed in their battle. It was a fight most people had to contend with daily—but only in their minds. But for Sam Beckett, suddenly what he wanted and what he desired had the chance to get at each other and could not be thwarted.

They continued to thrash, rolling under Ward's rig, so lost in the darkness that Al could not make out anything of their struggle. Fists flew up from the Sam on the bottom, down from the one on top. Cries of pain and screams of fury told the admiral nothing. Both voices were the same—sounded the same, said the same things.

One of the pair caught hold of the other's leg behind

the knee, then twisted it, digging into the soft flesh and nerves behind. The other Sam swung his fist blindly, connecting with his attacker's head. He felt the agonizing pressure release from his leg, saw what might have been a tooth go spitting through the air.

Punching in the code he needed for updates, Al read his handlink with dismay. Ziggy was feeding him one of the worst scenarios yet. According to the computer, no one was going to have to wait for an earthquake. Now Ziggy was predicting that there was a 58.9 percent chance that somehow the weapons would be released within the next fifteen minutes.

The sound of a slamming fist connecting with flesh came to his ears, and before Al could look away, the probability jumped to 63.4 percent . . .

".5, .8," he counted numbly as the numbers continued to climb, "65.2, .4, 70 . . ."

A kick connected with a resounding thud, followed by a gagging sound and another massive jump in Ziggy's readouts to 83.5. Al's face, shimmering in the reflected light of the handlink, hardened. Moving to the back of the barn where the two Sams had dragged their fight, he reached into the past for his deepest military bark, ordering, *"Stop this at once!"*

It was a good move, and well intentioned, but badly mistimed. One of the Sams had just gotten his hands around something long and smooth and clublike. Startled by Al's bellow, his swing went wild, missing its target and plowing through the unseen bottles and boxes stacked on a table at the back of the barn. Almost instantly, flames sprung up from the debris.

CHAPTER
TWENTY-SEVEN

"Sam," shouted Al. "What did you do?"

"I don't know," answered one of the Sams, maybe both.

Before any of the three could say anything else, though, the first small flames spread out and hit something wet and volatile. A small lake of flame shot across the table, dripping down onto the floor, licking at the wall behind.

"What in the name of any common sense were those idiots keeping in here?" moaned Al.

"Who knows?" one of the Sams said. "Who cares? With what these guys were up to, it could be anything. We've got to get out of here. Now!"

"The truck," shouted the other, backing away from the inferno of the barn's back wall. "We've got to get it out of here. Who knows what'll happen if the flames reach that crap they've got stored in it."

The two Sams came together, their outlines silhouetted by the growing fire. As the ancient planks of the barn surrendered to the spreading flames, Sam/Mark yelled, "We have to. Think—Sam. Think about yourself. We're the closest people to this stuff. If it goes off, it goes off with us right here."

Sam/Ward nodded, holding his hand over his mouth in the growing smoke.

"All right, I'm no fool," he said. "But I'm not hooked in. I'm going to have to back it into the link, and you're going to have to tell me if I made it."

"Right. Got it," answered his "brother," moving quickly to the space between the tractor and its trailer. Once there, however, he found that despite the growing illumination from the fire, he could not see clearly due to the angle. He shouted, "I can't see in there."

"I've got it," said Al, moving toward the Sam who had stayed behind, holding up his handlink. Walking directly through the truck, he held the link where it would shed its array of colored lights on the kingpin.

By that time, the other Sam had clambered back up into his cab. Once in place behind the wheel, he turned his key in the ignition and worked his way into gear, shouting over the sounds of the fire, "We've only got time for one try."

"So do it right the first time."

Sam/Ward moved his tractor forward slightly, then gently eased it into reverse, moving the multiple tons of vehicle backward as slowly as possible.

On the ground, Sam/Mark squinted his eyes, blinking often, trying to keep the thickening smoke from blinding him. He heard a dull metallic click and started for the front of the barn, shouting as he ran, "That's it! You got it. You got it. Now get that thing out of here."

Sam/Ward gunned the ton and a half of diesel motor, moving the tractor and trailer forward together. Bursting forth from the burning barn, he kept the rig moving, taking it a fast five hundred feet before he even began to think about arching back to pick up his other self.

In the barn, however, Sam had stayed behind to try to drag the two unconscious gunmen to safety. He'd been hurt fighting himself, however, and the heat was intense. As he fumbled with Eddie, the heavier of the two, Al shouted, "Sam, what're you doing? Those nozzles were going to kill you, remember? Leave 'em, leave 'em."

"Can't do it, Al," Sam/Mark wheezed, coughing at the same time. Hacking a dark ball of sooty phlegm onto his shirt, he gasped, "Can't go changing time now . . . can I?"

As he dragged the heavy man across the sand, both he and Al looked up in response to a noise from above. The roof had been swept by the fire and was already threatening to come down. Desperate, Sam/Mark stopped worrying about Eddie's comfort and pulled him along as fast as he could. Then, once he had the gunman outside the still standing doorway, he turned to go back inside for Skinner.

Something in the back of the barn exploded, sending arcs of flame shooting forward and upward. One blazed through Al, splashing against the far forward left corner of the barn. Droplets of flame rained down on Skinner, setting his clothes afire. Sam staggered over to the prone figure and threw himself atop it, using Mark Ralston's body to put out the flames. Then he pushed himself up and grabbed Skinner's wrists, dragging him across the sand as he had Eddie.

Just before he reached the door, however, Al yelled, "Sam! Duck!"

Without knowing why, but without hesitating, Sam dropped to the ground, landing on Skinner as a bullet passed over his falling body. Still aching all over, his eyes and lungs smarting from the smoke, he threw himself off the still unconscious gunman. Eddie was conscious and had his gun back. Another bullet tore up the sand inches from his body.

"Back, Sam," shouted Al, pointing toward the worst part of the fire. "Go back!"

Trusting Al, he did the unexpected and dodged backward. Eddie, who had been moving his hand in the other direction expecting Sam to break for freedom, wasted three shots trying to set down a killing spread pattern.

"Smart moves, Ralston. Whichever one you are," screamed the gunman over the roaring of the flames, over the ringing in his ears from his own gunfire. "But it don't matter—understand? I've got you now. You're dead meat, you son of a bitch! *Dead meat!*"

Sam/Mark circled around as Eddie finished screaming. He couldn't really hear Eddie, but the killer's intent was plain enough. The heat snapping out at Sam/Mark baked his skin. Blisters broke out on his back, his neck. He tried to stay away from the blazing back wall, but there was only so much distance between him and the end of Eddie's .45.

The gunman tried to train his sights on the constantly moving target. Eddie knew he only had one bullet left. He also knew that if he missed, he would never be able to reload before his intended victim could get to him.

Sam/Mark turned sideways directly into an unexpected burst of thick smoke jetting from a suddenly ignited oil can. The choking layer of heavy smog gagged him, stopping him in his tracks. It was only the delay of a handful of seconds, but it was all Eddie needed.

Swinging his arm in a killing arc, the gunmen stepped hard to brace his shot, whispering, "Time to go bye-bye, whoever you are."

Before he could pull the trigger, Ward's rig came sailing up the approachway to the barn, slamming Eddie aside and crashing through the madly raging inferno.

CHAPTER
TWENTY-EIGHT

"So," Sam said, staring at himself sitting in the next chair across the table, "if we did such a good job . . . why are we still here?"

"DamiFino," offered the Observer, rolling an unlit El Supremo around in his mouth. When both Sams turned and stared at him frowning deeply, he merely shrugged his shoulders.

"Sorry. I mean, hey, give me a break. When you talk about Leaping and I'm in the room, I figure you're talking to me."

"It's all right, Al," answered the Sam in Ward Ralston's body. "It's just, I mean, what else do we have to do in this Leap to get out of here?"

Grinning, the other Sam asked, "He's got a point, Al. What's Ziggy got to say about it, anyway?"

The admiral turned to his handlink. The lights from it flickered on and off in their usual irregular pattern, illuminating his face in pink—blue—orange—yellow—

"The Zig is as stumped as we are, boys. As best she can tell, everything should be perfect."

"Why?" asked Sam/Mark. "There must be something going on that we haven't fixed yet."

"Yeah, what more could we do?"

Sam/Ward put his feet up on the table in front of him. He was in no mood to care. He was in jail, trying to piece together what was happening with his "brother" during a half-hour visiting period.

So far, they had gone over what had happened twice, without being able to find any reason why they had not yet Leaped. With only a few minutes of their time together left, they ran down the points one by one, searching for something they might have overlooked. It did not seem promising.

Dr. Klein had arrived with what seemed to be all the police in the state. They had taken Skinner into custody. Eddie was still alive, but only barely. Working together, both Sams had been able to keep him breathing until the ambulances came. Sam/Mark told the police that he and his "twin" had planned all along to gather the evidence needed on Oregon R&T. When Klein looked stunned, Sam/Mark explained that he had told no one, fearing for his brother's safety.

Klein was not sure he believed his colleague. The police were sure they did not believe him, but they were willing to overlook it. The two Sams had been questioned separately, of course. But Al had moved back and forth between interrogation rooms and made sure that their stories matched reasonably. Besides that, the police, along with the federal agents who had moved in before the local authorities could even get everyone back to civilization, had the videotape, along with Sam/Ward's confession to having made other dumpings for OR&T. It was the accepted assumption of everyone involved that the courts would cut a small fish like him a basic immunity deal in exchange for his testimony against the corporation.

Sam/Mark was a hero to his college, his environmentalist friends, his students, the press, everyone. Sam/Ward had made an even greater impression on his wife and children. If they were behind him before, they were even more strongly for him now. Betty was more in love with him for doing the right thing—even if it meant his going to prison—than when she had first met him. Which put them all back at square one.

"I mean, damn," said Sam/Ward with frustration, "what else could we have to do, anyway? Everyone loves us, the bad guys are down for the count, Betty and the kids think I'm Clark Kent, or something. What's left to fix?"

"Does Ziggy have anything for us, Al?" asked the other Sam hopefully.

"I'm afraid not, Sam," answered the admiral, studying his handlink. "OR&T gets shut down within six months. The professor goes on teaching . . . and from the best our mechanical lady can see, even Ward and Betty keep it together. It seems the time that the two of them spent sharing one body changed both Ralstons, somehow. They started speaking again, and became more like real brothers."

Al stuck the handlink into his pocket. Folding his hands across his chest, he took in a deep breath, then let it go with a full sigh, adding, "You got me, boys."

The room went silent again, none of the three having anything more to add. The Sam not under arrest looked at his watch, showing it to his other self. Their time was slipping away quickly, and yet . . . they were not Leaping.

Then Al sat forward, sliding his hands over the surface of the desk between him and the two Sams as if he were actually touching it. Leaning toward them, he said, "Sam . . . suppose this Leap didn't have anything to do with the Ralston brothers?"

"What?"

"Al, what are you talking about? What else could we be here for? That's what this is all about. I Leap into someone, fix their life, and move on."

"Think about it, Sam," the Observer responded. "How long have you been doing this now? You're the greatest guy I know. The best friend I ever had. But even you can get tired of turning the other cheek—of always helping someone else and never yourself."

Swallowing hard, Al stared forward without blinking, and then dove ahead.

"What if this Leap was only partly to fix something with the Ralstons, Sam? What if this Leap was really for you?"

"Aw, look," answered Sam/Ward, pulling his feet off the table so he could sit forward as well. "I already said I'd go back to Leaping. It's not so bad. I mean, if nothing else, I like the part at the end, when I fill up with

226

that feeling that comes after I'm sure I've done the right thing.''

"You're saying it, Sam," said Al, certain he was on the right track, but with no way to prove it. "But do you mean it? Are you *sure*?"

"Of course I'm sure. I was sure when I said it before. The hell with stealing some other guy's life. I can lick this thing. If it takes twenty more years—I'll set things straight and I'll get back to the Project."

As always, Sam could not touch Al; could not shake his hand, clap him on the shoulder, anything. So, as he often did in the times he needed to convey feeling to his friend, he simply stared, opening his borrowed eyes to their fullest.

"I know I will, Al. I will."

"All well and good, Sam, but if you really do feel that way, then why aren't you Leaping?"

"Because," answered the other Sam, "I'm the one who's hesitating."

Al and Sam/Ward both turned toward Sam/Mark, surprise filling their faces. As they waited, the other Sam said, "I wanted to keep helping people—I did, I do. And at first, separated from"—he pointed toward his other self—"from, well, vested self-interest here, I really wanted to roll, Leaping on and on, never going back to the Project. But, but . . ."

"I know," said Sam/Ward, placing his hand on his brother's arm. "It's hard. Day after day, life after life . . . I know."

"We were wrong," the other Sam said quietly. "The Accelerator was a mistake. And this is our punishment.

We're going to be Leaping forever, all because I had to tinker with the universe."

"Maybe," Sam/Ward said, "and maybe not. Maybe it's our destiny. Whatever, it doesn't matter. How it happened, why it happened, neither one of us is responsible—we both are."

Sam/Mark lifted his head, searching in his brother's eyes for any sign of doubt. His own voice came out, full of confidence and strengthened belief.

"We'll see it all through until the end. We have to."

Tears streamed down both Sams' faces. The pent-up agonies and doubts he had been carrying with him since his first Leap suddenly began to break up like the icy top of a river on the first day of spring. As he hugged himself tightly, Al whispered to him, "Remember that good feeling you were talking about—the one you get when you're sure you've done the right thing? Something tells me it's about to set in."

Dazzling blue and white light poured forth from both Sams' bodies at once, beams cutting beams, shattering and magnifying each other with the spectral intensity of prisms. Shattering outward into violent purples, reds, and golds, the light swelled and then exploded once more, creating a sunrise there in the cell block, a display that immobilized Al for a moment.

It kept him stock still, speechless, unable to breathe until the last drizzling atom of it had faded away, leaving the real Ward and Mark Ralston behind where Sam had been a split second earlier; still holding each other, still crying.

228

And, as the Observer would admit to Sam much later, he had never seen his friend make a more beautiful Leap—a description that had little to do with the display that he alone had witnessed.